"What's so funny?"

Nola leaned in and playfully pushed at his chest. She didn't expect him to snake his arms around her waist and tug her flat against him.

"Mr. Langtry," Nola said in her best Scarlett O'Hara voice. "I do declare."

"I'm sorry, ma'am, but it's tradition," Chase replied with a pretty good Rhett Butler impression of his own.

"Tradition?"

"I do believe I spotted some mistletoe in this here tree earlier today."

"Mistletoe? Above us, right now?"

"Why, surely, ma'am. 'Tis the season and all. You wouldn't want to break a long-standing tradition now, would you?"

"No," Nola said. "I wouldn't want to do that."

A hairbreadth away, Chase moved even closer, his lips brushing hers. Afraid he'd pull back, Nola laced her fingers behind his neck and deepened their kiss. Her lips parted, inviting him in, not the least bit shy about having a taste of Chase for herself. So much for her earlier decision not to be brazen.

Dear Reader,

I am a firm believer that Christmas should be about family. When I began the Welcome to Ramblewood series, much of it centered around my own family, especially Joe Langtry, whose legacy is the driving force behind these books. Joe Langtry in real life was my Grandpa Joe, who died when I was sixteen. Writing about him and my Grandma Kay, who we lost a few years ago, helps me keep their memory alive.

Chase Langtry has been surrounded by family his entire life, especially around the holidays. While an over-the-top traditional Christmas was the norm for him, Nola West has never really celebrated the day, let alone experienced the weeks of festivities Ramblewood has planned.

Each of us has our own holiday traditions we pass down through the generations. Nola doesn't have any. As an outsider, she's taken aback by the sheer magnitude in which the entire town celebrates. She's a little hesitant at first, but who can resist some Ramblewood Christmas cheer?

Mistletoe Rodeo is the sixth book in the Welcome to Ramblewood series...where the door is always open.

Feel free to stop in and visit me at amandarenee.com. I'd love to hear from you.

Happy reading!

Amanda Renee

MISTLETOE RODEO

———

AMANDA RENEE

HARLEQUIN® AMERICAN ROMANCE®

ISBN-13: 978-0-373-75589-9

Mistletoe Rodeo

Copyright © 2015 by Amanda Renee

The publisher acknowledges the copyright holder
of the additional work:

A Home for Christmas
Copyright © 2005 Laura Marie Altom

Recycling programs
for this product may
not exist in your area.

Printed in U.S.A.

HARLEQUIN®
www.Harlequin.com

CONTENTS

MISTLETOE RODEO   7
Amanda Renee

A HOME FOR CHRISTMAS   229
Laura Marie Altom

Amanda Renee was raised in the Northeast and now wriggles her toes in the warm sand of coastal South Carolina. She was discovered through Harlequin's So You Think You Can Write contest and began writing for the Harlequin American Romance line. When not creating stories about love, laughter and things that go bump in the night, she enjoys the company of her schnoodle, Duffy, photography, playing guitar and anything involving horses. You can visit her at amandarenee.com.

Books by Amanda Renee

Harlequin American Romance

Welcome to Ramblewood

Betting on Texas
Home to the Cowboy
Blame it on the Rodeo
A Texan for Hire
Back to Texas

MISTLETOE RODEO

Amanda Renee

For Grandpa Joe

Your legacy lives on in each of us

Chapter One

Unbelievable!

Chase Langtry had thought the baseball cap and hoodie would be enough to elude overly ambitious reporter Nola West. He'd managed to dodge her for the past twenty-four hours, but now here she was standing in the aisle of his first-class cabin. Without even looking past her narrow waist and shapely hips, he knew it was her. Nola was tall, fit and taut in all the right places. Chase deemed himself an expert on her form, considering he'd been studying it for the past two and a half years, but the last thing he needed was to stare into her forget-me-not blue eyes. He'd be a goner for sure.

Scooting down farther in his seat and turning toward the window, Chase hoped Nola would get the message and leave him alone. He was tired, sore and still a bit hungover after blowing it in Las Vegas. Chase had headed into the National Finals Rodeo with a chance of winning it all. Only he'd reinjured his shoulder after his first ride had tossed him faster than tumbleweed in a tornado. And apparently his run of bad luck extended to his flight home because Nola settled in beside him, her arm brushing his.

The cords in his neck stiffened, aggravating his shoulder injury.

"Are you kidding me?" Chase straightened his spine and turned to confront her, immediately regretting the action when she lifted her face to his. She tucked a long strand of honey-blond hair behind one ear and narrowed her gaze.

"Geesh, I'm sorry. I didn't mean to encroach on your armrest space." Nola's sarcastic tone was all too evident. "I'll try to be more careful next time."

"That's not what I meant," Chase growled through clenched teeth, more frustrated than angry, thanks to the glimpse of bare thigh he'd just caught. "I'm talking about you—here—next to me—on this plane."

"Relax, Chase. We're flying home together—nothing more." Nola followed his eyes and tugged on her skirt hem.

"KWTT must really want this story if they're willing to upgrade you to first class. But let's get things straight—regardless of how nicely you ask, I'm not giving you an interview."

"I'm not asking for one." Nola fastened her seat belt and removed her iPad from her bag, paying Chase no further attention.

"No?" The porcelain glow of her skin caused Chase's fingers to ache, wanting to feel the softness of her cheek. He mentally kicked himself for allowing her presence to upset him. "You always look this stunning at two o'clock in the morning? Traveling in a skirt, high heels and full makeup?"

"You think I look stunning?" Nola glanced sideways at him. "Thank you…I think."

As if she didn't know how beautiful she was. Nola West was the last thing Chase needed right now. The past couple days had been bad enough, and now he had to endure four hours on a plane next to the woman he'd thought about almost daily since they'd met. It didn't help that her lips glimmered with newly applied gloss, which he thought definitely needed to be kissed off. Chase groaned inwardly.

"I'm willing to bet George has a handheld camera and microphone pack in his carry-on in case you snag an interview when we get off the plane."

"We cover the news." Nola didn't look at him, which only confirmed he was right. "We always travel prepared."

"Why'd you leave George in business class?" This was the first time he'd seen Nola without her everpresent cameraman sidekick. "Shame on you, and shame on the studio for not upgrading him, too."

"You're cranky and full of assumptions tonight, aren't you?" Nola glanced at him, one perfectly groomed brow arched higher than Chase would have thought possible.

"Not that I would expect you to notice, but there's a woman traveling with George and me on this trip. Unbeknownst to the studio, he brought his wife along—which we'd like to keep secret, if you don't mind. He wasn't about to upgrade his ticket to first class and leave her back there. Some people think of others, not just themselves."

Chase gripped his thighs. Was this a jab at him? Just because he was goal oriented didn't mean he was selfish. He fought to ignore Nola's comment. Getting into a war of words with her wouldn't make the flight any easier.

"I'd ask why you're not staying until the end of the competition, but I already know the answer. You're focused on my failure."

"You didn't fail, Chase." Nola huffed in the same exasperated tone Chase's mother used when her grandkids acted up. "You had a bad night. It happens to the best of them. You're right—I was in Vegas to cover you for the local news, and I'm leaving because you are."

"I can see the headline now." Chase sagged into the seat. "Hometown Hero Humiliated at National Finals Rodeo." He'd been pegged to win the World All-Around Champion Cowboy title.

"Was this a pity party? Because I forgot to bring a gift." Nola sighed. "It's not the end of the world. You've known me for a while now. Have I ever cast you in a bad light? No, I haven't. I've always covered you and your family in a respectful way. Besides, I can spin the story so it doesn't look as bad as it really is. Wait—I didn't mean it like that."

Nola reached for his arm but he shook her off. He didn't want anyone's pity. "I know exactly what you meant."

Chase watched the lights of the Vegas strip fade as

the plane lifted off. He was heading home a failure, and no matter how Nola *spun* the story, it wouldn't change the fact that he'd blown it. His entire hometown of Ramblewood, Texas, had counted on him to bring home the coveted championship belt buckle. And not only had he not won, but he also had left the competition early. He could thank his stubbornness for leading him straight to a disastrous finish on day two. Chase had known when he'd pulled the ligaments in his shoulder two weeks earlier that he should have bowed out of the competition. But too many people had invested in him, and he'd refused to let them down. His doctors had cautioned him that one more injury could end his career. And yesterday's ride had probably done just that.

His older brother, Shane, hadn't helped matters by constantly pushing Chase into the spotlight. The World All-Around title had been Shane's dream, but he'd given up his own chance to compete so he could devote more time to his son's rodeo schedule. In the end, Chase could've said no, but he hadn't, and there was no one to blame except himself.

Chase and Shane jointly owned the state-of-the-art Ride 'em High! Rodeo School. Having a world champion on the roster would've been great for business. Not that they were in need of more students; since their doors opened a few years ago, the school has been booked full every session. Chase felt as if he'd failed not only his family this week but his students, too.

As if things hadn't been bad enough already,

sitting next to Nola—as savvy as she was sexy—unnerved him more than the final seconds atop a bull before the chute gate swung open. Chase was determined not to let her get the better of him.

"I spoke to your mom before she flew home yesterday," Nola said. "Regardless of what happened in the competition, she's really proud of you."

"You interviewed my mom?" Chase shoved his hoodie back and faced her. Going after him for an interview was one thing—his family was another.

"Of course not." Nola met his gaze, her annoyance evident. "I saw her in the lobby as she was leaving."

The lengths reporters went to in order to get a story irritated Chase. But Nola's pursuit tried his patience even more and he wasn't sure why. "In other words, you were stalking me in the lobby—waiting for me to come down. I bet if I ask my mother, she'd confirm that George was by your side."

"He was." Nola ran her palms slowly down the front of her skirt. "And I *was* waiting for you, but it was out of concern. You took a hard hit out there. When you got injured, I genuinely cared."

Nola's words softened with her admission. Chase swallowed hard, afraid he'd say too much. "The only thing injured is my pride," Chase lied and turned back to the window. "Thank you for your concern."

"Don't mention it." The natural lilt of her voice returned. "Your mom is really excited about Christmas this year. All the grandkids must be getting big. I haven't seen them in a year, at least. I bet your house is packed over the holidays."

There lay the other reason Chase hated to go home. He'd considered changing his flight to meet up with some of his friends in Cancun, but the thought had been short-lived. Once his mother had gotten wind of it she'd threatened to tan his hide. In the Langtry household, Christmastime was family time. Every year his mother would decorate the ranch from the entrance to the stables in a display guaranteed to delight the electric company. The rest of Ramblewood had nothing on her. She'd even spread the holiday spirit to the stables by placing small wreaths on each of the stall doors and insisting on red or green halters and blankets for the horses. Once night fell, the ranch glowed so brightly that he and his brothers swore it must be visible from outer space.

Chase loved his family, but they were a constant reminder of what he didn't have—a wife and kids of his own. With his wealth and status, it had become increasingly difficult to tell if a woman was interested in him or his bank account. It always hit him harder this time of year, especially now that all of his brothers were married with children. The irony of the situation was that none of his brothers had even wanted to settle down. Chase, however, had always envisioned a house full of children running around, much like the one he grew up in.

Chase hated to admit it, but he was envious of his three older brothers. Their children were their greatest accomplishments. Jesse and Miranda's twins, Jackson and Slade, had turned two this past July; his niece Ever was seven; and his fifteen-year-old nephew, Hunter, was well on his way to becoming a champion rodeo competitor himself. By the time Chase got around to having children, their cousins would be married with kids of their own.

Turning thirty in a couple of days only added to his frustration. Chase wished he'd said yes to Cancun and was headed to Mexico rather than sitting next to a woman he'd much rather ask to dinner than argue with. But a date with Nola was out of the question. She had an air of worldly sophistication about her and would surely prefer someone who had a lot more going on than a rodeo cowboy, regardless of his wealth. Besides, the only time Chase ever saw her was when he or his family were part of her news coverage. No, the attraction was definitely one-sided.

"Please don't take this personally, but I'm not up for talking tonight." It was better to end the conversation now before he became even more aggravated.

Nola shrugged and refocused her attention on her screen. Chase popped in his earbuds and turned up the volume of his iPod, drowning out the world around him. Closing his eyes as he settled against the seat, he pulled his hat down lower.

Nola deserved better than his ornery attitude. If he hadn't found the reporter so attractive, maybe he could find a way to be more cordial to her. But that was the problem—she was a journalist above all else, and anything he did or said would appear in her next story. Nola West made no apologies for her persistent climb up the network ladder, and Chase refused to be one of those rungs.

The woman was too perfectly poised. Chase would like to get her dirty—show her what it felt like to be out of her element and relinquish control to someone else. If circumstances were different, he'd love to help her find her wild side for an hour or two. He gave his head a shake. Nola needed to remain off-limits.

REPORTING FROM THE side of a war-torn highway in Kuwait had been easier than tracking down Chase Langtry in Nevada. He'd managed to avoid her at every turn. Her studio had shelled out big bucks for Nola to secure the interview, although they had anticipated it would be about a local cowboy making good. Once her news director had heard of Chase's disastrous ride, he'd dangled the upcoming KWTT co-anchor position in front of Nola. He had warned her if she ever expected to get anywhere in this business, she had better start bringing in some harder-hitting stories. The rise and fall of the rodeo star was a start.

When she had seen Chase drowning his sorrows in the hotel bar last night, she'd felt a tinge sorry for him—but it had been short-lived. Based on everything her cousin Kylie had told her about the Langtrys, the four brothers had had their lives, and then some, handed to them on a silver platter. The famously rich "First Family of Ramblewood" had it all. If losing the championship at the National Finals Rodeo was the worst thing that had happened to Chase, then he needed to count his blessings. She'd seen people take some serious knocks in life, and losing a rodeo competition didn't even come close.

Nola had first interviewed Chase and the Langtry family two and a half years ago at the grand opening of the Ride 'em High! Rodeo School and Dance of Hope Hippotherapy Center. While Nola had simply adored the mother, Kay, she'd thought the brothers were a little over-the-top and too entitled.

"Would you care for a drink?" a flight attendant asked.

"Scotch, please." No girly drinks for Nola. She'd learned how to drink around military men, and unless it burned on the way down, it didn't classify as a drink.

They both looked at Chase when he didn't respond, but he was oblivious with his headphones tucked firmly in place. After a quick nudge from Nola's elbow, Chase turned the music down long enough to order a bourbon and then quickly resumed sulking in the corner.

Nola had known Chase would travel first class and had convinced her news director, Pete, to approve her ticket upgrade only to discover she was seated a few rows behind the cowboy. After a little flirtation with the man originally assigned to her seat, Nola had managed to finagle her way beside Chase.

If he'd remove those damn things from his ears and talk to her, she might have something worth reporting. A brooding cowboy didn't make much of a headline, but a man battling his inner demons might be enough to satisfy both the station and Chase. After all, there were two sides to every story, but Chase needed to open up in order for Nola to save his reputation and possibly his wounded pride.

So Nola did what her seven years in the Army had trained her to do. She improvised. When the flight attendant handed Nola her drink, she purposely bumped it so it spilled on Chase's iPod.

"Oh, you're good." Chase pushed back his ball cap, exposing more of his tousled blond hair. He stared at her with a piercing turquoise glare that would've intimidated most people, but Nola had covered the news from the landmine-ridden Persian Gulf countryside and had witnessed the other side of evil. Chase didn't come close.

"I've got to hand it to you, Nola—I didn't see that one coming."

Nola had to hand it to *him*. He didn't get mad or even swear. He just quietly tossed everything into an airline barf bag, earbuds and all.

"It was an accident." Nola fought to squelch her guilt. "Don't you carry a spare iPod with you?"

"No, I don't carry a spare iPod with me," Chase mocked. "Who would? And please don't play coy. I don't believe that was an accident. You're too precise and calculating for that to happen."

Nola recoiled at his remark, though it wasn't completely off base. She had learned to maintain discipline out of necessity and survival. There had been a time in her life when Reckless was her middle name.

"Okay, you have my attention." Chase dabbed at his jeans with the tissues she handed him from her bag. "What do you want to talk about? I already told you no interviews, so I hope you don't think *this* will change anything."

"Do you have any plans for the holidays?" Nola had covered Chase enough times to know the way to his heart was through his family. "I bet Kay goes all out, doesn't she?"

"Even more now that she has the grandkids around." Chase's broad shoulders relaxed a bit and he settled back as he spoke, confirming to Nola that she knew how to read her interviewees. "It's not only my mother, though. The entire town goes a little overboard," Chase said drily. "Haven't you ever been to Ramblewood over the holidays?" He paused. "I just realized I don't know where you live."

"I have a small condo in Willow Tree." Even though she only lived a half hour from Ramblewood, Nola purposely avoided the town during the holidays despite Kylie's best efforts to persuade her to join the annual festivities.

"Willow Tree, really? Nice place. You know, you've interviewed me a dozen times and I know absolutely nothing about you. Let's try this a different way. If you're game, why not let me have the honor of interviewing you for the rest of the flight home?"

Nola wasn't used to someone turning the tables on her and it made her a tad uncomfortable. That and the fact that her Spanx was cutting off her air supply. She didn't normally wear the Lycra from hell when she traveled. Standing in it was bad enough, never mind sitting for hours, but she had put it on anticipating an interview when they landed. The camera really did add ten pounds.

Beads of sweat began to form across her forehead. Not many people knew Nola the person. It was the nature of the job—she asked the questions, not the other way around. Nola's growing attraction to the bachelor cowboy compounded her discomfort. The close quarters only added to her interest in the man. Chase grinned and Nola found herself unable to say no.

"Fine." Nola shrugged and braced herself. "Ask me anything you want. It's only fair."

"How did you know I'd be on this flight?"

Nola laughed, expecting a completely different line of questioning. "It was a hunch. I figured you'd want to avoid everyone back home, so you'd book a red-eye flight. Looks as if I was right."

"Your perception is dangerous." Chase's smile told her he was teasing but his deep, throaty voice hinted at its own danger.

"You have no idea how dangerous I can be," she answered. *What am I doing?* Flirting with an interviewee was not a good idea. It wasn't forbidden, but it wasn't professional, either.

"I know Kylie and your aunt and uncle, but I don't remember you when we were growing up. Is your family from Texas?"

"My family is from everywhere," Nola answered. "I was raised in the Army, born in New Orleans—my name is an acronym for New Orleans, Louisiana— and I've lived in seventeen different countries and can speak eight languages rather fluently."

"I'm impressed. So you're a military brat?" Chase nodded and smiled, a hint of laughter bubbling underneath. "That explains your *precise and calculating* nature."

"Well, that and the fact that I've served in the Army myself. I did three tours on the front lines and I'm still on inactive duty for the next year."

Nola enjoyed watching the smile slide from Chase's face. She wanted to tell herself that it didn't matter what he thought, but it stung a bit to know he wasn't the least bit interested in her. If he had been, he would've taken the time to read her bio on KWTT's website. Nola's military past was all there.

"I had no idea." Chase flagged down a flight attendant. "May I have another round of drinks for myself and my traveling companion here?"

The flight attendant quickly returned with fresh glasses of ice and tiny airline bottles. "What are you doing?" Nola asked.

Twisting off the tops of both, Chase poured the amber liquid into their glasses. He lifted his in the air. "Here's to you, soldier. Thank you for your commitment and sacrifice for our country."

"Thank you." Nola touched her glass to his. "If I didn't know better, I'd say you were trying to get me drunk. This is my limit. I have to drive home once we land."

"Maybe I just wanted to relax you enough that you'd stop thinking about the interview you're not going to get." Chase laughed. "In all seriousness, though, Nola, I applaud your bravery. When I was in high school I considered enlisting, but I chickened out. What division were you in?"

Chase's admiration should have flattered Nola, and it would have if she had joined the Army willingly. But it had been either the Army or jail, and the military had seemed like a much better option.

"You mean what division am I *in*. I'm a public affairs broadcast specialist, and they can call me to active duty at any time."

"Are you scared?"

Nola detected genuine concern in Chase's voice, and the unexpected tug at her heart knocked her slightly off-balance.

"Believe me—I understand the definition of the word *scared*. When I was in the Middle East, I covered the most gruesome stories you could imagine. Aside from that, active duty would derail my career. By law, the studio has to hold my position, but that doesn't mean they won't find someone better in the meantime. I can receive new orders with only a couple of days' notice to get my affairs in order and be ready to go. Yes, it makes me nervous, especially whenever I hear they're sending more troops overseas. I'm sure I'll remain that way until Thanksgiving Day next year."

Once that day finally rolled around, Nola's sentence would be complete. At least the physical one. She'd have to live with the reality of what she'd done—the life she'd taken—forever.

AN UNSETTLED FEELING washed over Chase when Nola mentioned that active duty was a real possibility. A softened, unsteady tone replaced the matter-of-fact, in-control voice she usually had. He felt like a moron.

"Are you smirking?" Nola asked, slightly defensive.

"I have a confession. When you sat down earlier, I thought how nice it would be to get you dirty and show you what real work was like. Now I'm thinking you could not only teach me a thing or two, but you could probably kick my ass."

"I'll drink to that." Nola raised her glass. "And yes, I probably could."

The more she told him about her army life, the more Chase forgot she was a reporter. She was easy to talk to.

"Is your family stateside?" Chase felt like a fool for not knowing more about Nola. It wasn't as if he hadn't had the opportunity over the past year. She'd covered every local event he'd been in and she'd been out to his family's ranch numerous times. But he'd always been the focus of the conversation. Chase cringed. Nola was right—he had only been thinking of himself.

"My parents are stationed in the Netherlands and my brother is in Germany with his family. I have nieces and nephews I've never met. We lived in Texas for a year when I was in high school. Of all the places we'd been stationed, it was my favorite. With the Army's assistance, I completed my education and took a position at KWTT."

There it was again. A touch of sadness, only this time it appeared when she spoke of her family. Chase couldn't fathom not having his ever-multiplying and perpetually boisterous relatives nearby.

"I bet the holidays were exciting when you were growing up." Chase attempted to lighten the mood. "With you living among different cultures and traditions and all."

"They were anything but." Nola shifted in her seat, seemingly a little uncomfortable with his line of questioning. Chase wondered if that was how he appeared when he was interviewed. "We didn't see my father for months at a time, sometimes longer, and I can only remember a handful of Christmases where we were all together. Mom was usually depressed over the holidays, so they weren't a big deal to us kids."

Chase turned farther in his seat to face her. Despite her indifferent tone, he noticed a slight pulsation in her jaw. Christmas should be a happy occasion for every child. "Tell you what, I'll grant you an interview if you focus on the Mistletoe Rodeo and the charity auction instead of me."

Chase thought it was a cardinal sin that Nola hadn't experienced an old-fashioned Texas Christmas. If he kept himself occupied with showing her some down-home holiday spirit, maybe he wouldn't feel so lonely this year. Besides, who didn't love a good Christmas story? Her viewers should eat it up.

"You want me to do a feature about a Christmas show?" Nola looked down at her hands. "No offense, but in the industry, we call that a puff piece."

Not quite the response Chase had expected, but he was quickly learning that nothing with Nola was predictable.

Chase winced as pain crept into his shoulder again. At this rate, he doubted if he'd even be able to perform in the Mistletoe Rodeo in a couple of weeks. Although it was only an exhibition event, Chase needed to be in much better condition before he could even consider it. As it stood, he was potentially facing surgery.

"How bad is it?" Nola asked as Chase rubbed his shoulder.

"I pulled ligaments a few weeks ago and it still hasn't fully healed." Chase nonchalantly lowered his hand, afraid Nola would pick up too much from his discomfort. His doctor had prescribed pain relievers, but he wasn't a big fan. He hated the side effects, preferring pain to the feeling of being out of sorts, especially when on top of a one-ton animal.

"You competed injured?" Nola asked. "Why would you take the risk?"

He ground his teeth. "Nola, we agreed not to discuss this."

"This is strictly off the record," Nola insisted. "Does your family know? Did your team and your sponsors think it was a good idea?"

"This wasn't exactly my first rodeo," Chase countered. "I'm also smart enough to know nothing is ever off the record when it comes to the media."

They sat in silence for the next few minutes. Chase was tired of the constant scrutiny he received from the news outlets, but that was what the rodeo was about—someone was always judging your performance. Chase had made his decision the moment he'd hit the dirt facedown in the middle of the Thomas & Mack Center arena. It was time to retire and devote his attention to the rodeo school and his family's ranch.

"Nola, I'm sorry. I've had a rough couple of days and I'm taking it out on you. You don't deserve it."

"No, I understand. I came after you like a barracuda. I didn't mean to insult you with my puff piece comment, either." Nola rested her hand on his. The warmth of her touch made him instantly grateful they weren't alone. As luxurious as flying first class was, it was far from a romantic setting. "The station expects me to come back with a story and I don't have one. Sugarplums and mistletoe won't cut it, but if you let me tell them you fought through the pain and were determined not to let your hometown down, it would put you in a better light."

Chase withdrew his hand and faced the darkened window. "Does it really look that bad?"

"It's not that it looks bad. It just—it could be better if you let me spin it."

Chase squeezed his eyes shut. He wanted nothing more than to find a way to ease the disappointment his hometown felt over his loss. "Why should I trust you?"

"Oh, Chase, why shouldn't you? I'm not out to hurt you and this is the nightly news, not TMZ. I'll tell you what." Chase heard Nola's nails click against her iPad screen. Curiosity got the better of him and he faced her again. "What if I agree to cover the Mistletoe Rodeo and you allow me to do a brief interview about how you were injured before the competition? And just to prove to you that we won't take anything you say out of context, we'll do an interview when we land. It will be a lead-in to the Mistletoe Rodeo story."

When Chase had suggested the Mistletoe Rodeo and charity auction to Nola, he'd hoped to deflect the community's attention away from his recent failure. But he knew that avoiding the subject wouldn't make the town forget it happened. Spending time with Nola was either an unexpected bonus or a curse. He hadn't quite made up his mind yet.

"I guess that's fair enough, but no interviews when we land. How about you and George come out to the ranch tomorrow—well, later today, at this point—and Lord willing we'll get an interview with my mother since she's chairing the event. She seemed at ease with the other interviews you've conducted with her, so it shouldn't take too much persuading, although she may shoot me for the short notice. Too bad school's still in session or I'd tell George to bring his children along with him. Maybe I'll even put you to work with the horses."

"You're not going to make this easy on me, are you?" Nola's laugh was contagious. Chase had to keep his head straight and remind himself this visit was for an interview and nothing more.

"For a military girl like you, a day at the ranch

should be a cakewalk. I expect you to be in jeans tomorrow—not all perfectly coiffed."

"Coiffed?" Nola snickered.

"Hey, my sisters-in-law have taught me a thing or two about the female persuasion."

"You've got a deal, cowboy." Nola offered her hand and they shook on it.

Chase held on longer than he probably should have, but he suddenly found himself looking forward to the holidays at home. He was aware that Nola had only agreed to cover the Mistletoe Rodeo, but in that moment, he had an incredible desire to show her a Christmas she'd never forget.

Chapter Two

Nola dreaded the holidays. They were lonely and de-pressing. One of the drawbacks of military life was that most of Nola's friends were scattered through-out the world. Even though her cameraman, George, had said she was more than welcome to join them for the holidays, she didn't want to intrude on his family time. His wife was cordial enough, but Nola got the distinct impression Betty would prefer her husband spend a little less time around his female colleague.

When their plane touched down, the reality of what she'd agreed to began to set in. More time with Chase Langtry meant having to endure an extended Hall-mark moment at the Bridle Dance Ranch. His home life was sweet, touching and idyllic, and Nola wanted it for herself. In all her travels, she'd never met people like the Langtrys. No matter how many times she had interviewed them, she always walked away yearning for a place to call home and a family with which to share her celebrations.

It wasn't only Christmas—it was birthdays and anniversaries, too. Being alone was hard, and while she had some family relatively nearby, they hadn't been close when Nola was growing up. She felt like an outsider every time she visited.

After agreeing to meet George later for their interview at Bridle Dance, Nola said goodbye to him and Betty. Chase walked with her to the parking area but stopped abruptly and looked around.

"What's wrong?" Nola asked. "Did you forget where you parked?"

"No." Chase took off his ball cap and raked his hand through his hair before tugging his cell phone from his pocket. "I forgot that when I sent Shane and my mother home ahead of me, I told them to take the Navigator. I guess I'll call car service."

"Chase, you live more than an hour away from here. Let me give you a ride home."

"I can't ask you to do that." Chase scrolled through his phone.

"Why not? I have to drive past Ramblewood anyway. Come on. I won't take no for an answer."

Nola continued walking toward her car, not bothering to wait for Chase. She figured he'd eventually follow. Waiting for car service was ridiculous when they were headed in the same direction.

"You have to let me pay for the gas, at least." She heard the sound of Chase's boots trudging after her.

"Deal."

The sun rose over the interstate, creating what Nola deemed a romantic ambiance inside her vintage red Volkswagen Beetle. When Nola was a girl, she had fantasized about riding in an old pickup truck with a bench seat and a cowboy at the wheel, his arm draped across her shoulders. She didn't need a knight in shining armor—her fairy tale was much simpler. Not that Chase could be a part of that fairy tale. He was definitely eye candy, and when he wasn't grumpy from losing, he was generally pleasant to talk with. But he also came from a respectable family—one that wouldn't want anything to do with her past.

"I'm sure you're tired, but would you allow me to buy you breakfast as a thank-you?" Chase broke into her thoughts.

"I could eat," Nola agreed. "Where did you have in mind?"

"The Magpie?"

Of course. Instead of somewhere less cozy like the Waffle House, it was just like Chase to choose the quintessential luncheonette in the heart of the quintessential town. She loved the quirky little place, but whenever she left it, she found herself yearning for something she didn't have. Nola didn't want to be that person who always wanted more. She was grateful for what she had in life—especially the second chance she'd been given.

"The Magpie sounds wonderful."

Once they arrived and Chase had endured a couple rounds of "you'll win it next year," they slid into the booth farthest away from everyone's stares.

"Are you sure you want to stay here?" Nola asked.

"I promised you breakfast, and I keep my promises."

Nola glanced around, feeling as if they'd time-warped into a Christmas episode of *Happy Days*. The fifties-style luncheonette was draped from top to bottom in holiday kitsch. Festive songs played merrily in the background while glittery garlands danced above archways. Little Christmas trees were tucked wherever there was a free corner and snow globes decorated every table. The waitresses wore red dresses with white aprons and Santa hats, and Nola could swear she spotted the cook in an elf costume. She couldn't help but wonder what the rest of the places in town looked like inside. Chase wasn't kidding when he said everyone went all out.

Over a breakfast of gingerbread-flavored coffee and eggnog pancakes, Chase practically had Nola in tears as he described the previous Christmas morning when his mother's dog, Barney, had attempted to climb the fully decorated tree.

"The poor thing must have thought it was one giant squeaky toy." Chase laughed. "Everything toppled over, but luckily the presents cushioned the fall and very few ornaments broke. This year Mom said she's anchoring the tree to the wall with fishing line."

Nola couldn't remember the last time she'd put up a tree. There was no sense in having one in her condo when no one else was there to enjoy it.

"I bet there's never a dull moment in your house." Nola's family life had been just the opposite. Nola and her brother had never been allowed to play inside or make any noise. Children were to be seen and not heard in the West household. Having a lieutenant general for a father meant always having to be an example for other children on base.

"The Ramblewood Winter Festival is this weekend. You should come," Chase said. "It would be a great opportunity to interview some people about the Mistletoe Rodeo."

"Oh, I don't know." As much as she appreciated the invitation, Nola feared she'd feel out of place in what she considered a family event. "I don't want to intrude. Thank you, but I'll pass."

"Nonsense." Chase reached for her hands across the table and held them in his own. "It's no intrusion. There's no such thing as an outsider in Ramblewood. Everyone's welcome. Promise me you'll think about it."

Nola stared down at their hands. His warmth was comforting, the invitation tempting. Between the flight and the drive from the airport, Chase had unexpectedly managed to charm his way through Nola's outer shell, which was no small feat. When she had wormed her way beside him in first class, she'd had a completely different agenda in mind. Now she found herself more interested in the man than the story she was pursuing. She couldn't afford to blur those lines.

The problem was, a Christmas piece wouldn't help Nola secure the co-anchor position on the KWTT Evening News. It was between her and Dirk Stevens, another on-the-scene reporter. Dirk was good, but Nola was determined to be better, to make sure that it was her name they would announce for the position on New Year's Day. It may not be the big leagues, but at twenty-five years old, it was a step in the right direction toward the ultimate victory: a job at CNN. She'd just have to focus on her work and dig elsewhere for an award-winning story. There was no time to daydream about Chase Langtry.

CHASE CAUGHT A ride home with his sister-in-law after he ran into her at The Magpie. It should have dawned on him earlier that she might be there since her mother owned the place. Even though he'd been tempted to spend a few extra minutes with Nola, he was relieved at Tess's arrival.

As he entered the house, Chase heard humming and was surprised when he realized it was his own voice. Nola had succeeded in relieving his apprehension about facing everyone, if only for a little while. He was immediately ambushed by his mother's black standard poodle and took a moment to give Barney some playful pets before making his way upstairs.

Chase closed his bedroom door, kicked off his clothes and jumped into the shower, eager to wash away the remains of the flight and quell his thoughts of Nola.

He was the last of his four siblings to remain in their childhood home. That wasn't to say some of them hadn't still been living there into their thirties, But Chase had become more conscious of it now that his birthday was looming.

After their father's death a few years back, the brothers had collectively decided to remain on the ranch so their mother wouldn't feel so alone in the stately house. As his brothers married, they left the house one by one, leaving only Chase and Kay. When his rodeo schedule kept him on the road, his brothers would arrange for the grandkids to sleep over. His mother knew what they were up to, but she didn't complain. She welcomed the company. During the day, the brothers, their wives and their children filled the house with laughter, but the nights were deafeningly quiet once everyone left.

After a shower and change of clothes, Chase was surprisingly alert. He didn't know if he was still amped up from his disastrous showing in Las Vegas, or if it was the anticipation of Nola coming to the ranch that afternoon.

"I thought I heard you come in." His mother greeted him as he entered the kitchen. "We weren't sure when you'd return. How are you doing?"

"I'm surviving. Sore more than anything." Chase gave his mother a hug. "But I still don't want to talk about it. I do have something to ask you, though."

"Whenever one of you boys begins a sentence that way, I know I'm in trouble." Kay pulled out a kitchen chair and sat with her hands folded in her lap, waiting for a bomb to drop.

"Mom, it's not bad." Chase eased into a chair across from her. "Nola West is coming here this afternoon to ask you a few questions about the Mistletoe Rodeo and charity auction. Are you willing to do an on-camera interview?"

Kay's eyes narrowed suspiciously. "When did you

and Nola have a conversation? The last I saw, you couldn't get away from her fast enough."

"We ended up sitting next to each other on the flight home."

"Uh-huh." Kay continued to scrutinize him. "I think there's more to the story than you're telling me, but I'll agree to an interview. I've always liked Nola. And I've always liked her for you."

Chase rolled his eyes. "Mom, please don't play matchmaker."

"Why not? You could use some romance in your life." Kay rose and pushed in her chair. "Well, I guess I should find something to wear."

Chase shook his head and stood. "Nola's not coming until later this afternoon. You have plenty of time." He helped himself to a freshly baked apple-pecan muffin from a plate on the counter. "Please promise me you won't try to push Nola and me together." Chase thought his mother was about to argue with him when he caught a glint in her eyes. "What are you up to?"

"Nothing, dear. Let me go get myself camera ready. It takes me longer these days, you know."

As his mom headed upstairs, Chase headed outside. Not willing to face any of the rodeo school students just yet, Chase bypassed the indoor arena and made his way to the ranch's main office in the stables. Every time he walked through the entrance of what his father had affectionately called the horse mansion, Chase swore he could still hear the man's laughter. This would be their fourth Christmas without Joe Langtry. People said it would get better with time, but it hadn't. You learned to deal with the pain and move on, but it never seems to get any better.

The Bridle Dance offices were on the second level of the arts-and-crafts style building. Halfway up the open staircase, Chase stopped and looked around. The building had four quadrants, and from his vantage point he could survey each corridor of his father's masterpiece. The ranch, originally only a handful of acres, had been a wedding gift from his great-grandfather to his great-grandmother. Chase's eldest brother, Cole, and his wife, Tess, lived in the original cottage. Over the decades, the Langtrys had expanded the property into a quarter-of-a-million-acre estate. Today, Bridle Dance was one of the state's largest paint and quarter cutting horse ranches.

His father had retired from the rodeo the day before Cole was born. Now the time had come for Chase to make that decision—the hardest of his life. He felt he owed it to his family to devote more time to the business. Hopefully everything else would fall into place soon after.

Chase climbed the remainder of the stairs and was relieved to find Cole alone. He cleared his throat.

"Hey."

Cole spun around in his chair. "I didn't expect to see you until much later. I'm surprised you're still awake." He rose and gave Chase a manly, back-patting hug.

"So am I." Chase walked over to one of the windows overlooking the ranch. "Do you have a minute?"

"Sure." Cole fixed two cups of coffee in the office's minikitchen and handed one to his younger brother. Chase appreciated not being drilled about Las Vegas. A former rodeo rider himself, Cole was familiar with the disappointment of not winning.

Being the eldest of the four Langtry brothers, Cole had become the patriarch of the family since their father's death, and Chase wanted to discuss his decision with him before he told anyone else. He took a seat across from Cole.

"That was my last competitive ride." The relief of actually saying the words was greater than he had anticipated. "The doctors warned me a few weeks ago that I wouldn't be able to recover from too many more injuries. I'd rather walk away than be told I can't compete anymore. I already know there's a good chance I'll need surgery on my shoulder if the physical therapy doesn't help this time."

"I can't say I blame you for wanting to make the decision yourself," Cole said. "Do you know what you want to do next?"

"I'm going to continue with the school, of course. Shane could use a break after carrying my weight all this time. But I also want to put in more time here at the ranch. I haven't been able to do it before and it's important to me to be a part of Dad's legacy."

"There's certainly plenty of work to go around." Cole sipped his coffee. "Have you spoken to your agent or your sponsors about this yet?"

"No. I wanted to talk to you first. I don't even know where to begin."

Chase wasn't just walking away from the rodeo—he was walking away from multiple paychecks from the various companies sponsoring him. Luckily, his agent was firm on only signing year-to-year contracts. This being the end of the rodeo season, Chase was free and clear to walk away.

"Financially you're okay since the balance of your trust comes due on your thirtieth birthday. Call your agent and tell him your decision, but give yourself a couple days before you do. You may even want to wait until after the holidays. Once you tell him, he'll talk to your publicist and they'll handle it from there. Be prepared for an onslaught of phone calls. Walking away isn't easy."

"Neither is telling Shane." Chase still wasn't sure how he was going to break it to him. "He's been living vicariously through me for the past two years."

"Shane walked away from the rodeo, too. Granted he didn't have an injury hanging over his head, but he did it midseason and there were quite a few repercussions surrounding his decision. You have my support, but I mean it when I say take the holidays to come to terms with this and be a hundred percent positive this is what you want before you announce it publicly. Enjoy some downtime for a change."

Downtime was a foreign concept to Chase. Between the rodeo and the school, he found himself run ragged most of the time. With a handful of days left to this year's final session, Chase looked forward to a lighter workload. When his mom had asked him to cochair the Mistletoe Rodeo, Chase had hesitated at first and then decided it wouldn't be so bad working alongside his mother. Over the past few months, he'd helped organize many of the events leading up to the charity auction at the end of the evening. To his surprise, he had enjoyed every minute of it.

"Nola West is coming to the ranch later this afternoon to interview Mom and me about the Mistletoe Rodeo. Do you want to be a part of it?"

"Tess mentioned she saw you two together at The Magpie. I have to tell you, when Shane came home from Vegas he said watching you and Nola was like watching Wile E. Coyote chase the Road Runner."

"I bet it was." Chase laughed. "She was a bit relentless and even wrangled a seat next to me on the plane. Did you know she served three tours in the Middle East?"

"No, I didn't, but I guess it means she's capable of taking on a Langtry man."

Chase almost dropped his mug. "What's that supposed to mean?"

Cole eyed him skeptically. "It's obvious the woman has a thing for you, and the way you pant over her when she's not looking leads me to believe the feeling's mutual."

"I do not." Chase stood and dumped the remainder of his coffee in the sink, not daring to look at his brother.

"Yeah, okay. Whatever you say. I don't have time for an interview, though. Do me a favor and run these to the lab for me. Lexi should be down there somewhere. Just don't take the coward's way out and have her tell Shane your decision. He deserves to hear this from you."

Cole knew Chase too well. For a split second, he had contemplated just that—asking Lexi to break the news to her husband. Chase was a rodeo cowboy, and he wasn't sure if he knew how to be anything else. How would the school fare having two "retired has-beens" who'd never won the World All-Around as owners? That win spoke·volumes in the industry and, once again, Chase felt like he'd let everyone down.

"WHERE'S THE STORY?" Pete Devereaux, KWTT's news director, boomed through the phone.

"I don't have it yet." Nola tried to think of a way to tell Pete he wasn't going to get the type of story he had expected. "I'm meeting Chase at Bridle Dance this afternoon."

"We sent you all the way to Las Vegas and back— first class, I might add—and you still don't have anything. If we wanted you to get the story at the ranch, we could've saved ourselves a lot of money."

"I know." Nola's voice went dry. "He refused to give me an interview in the airport. I wasn't going to hound him like a tabloid reporter. It's not my style. Besides, the interview at the ranch was his idea."

"Of course it was. You'll be on his home turf," Pete grunted. "You've got to bring me something good if you want this co-anchor job. Dirk just locked down an exclusive tell-all interview with Senator Waegle about the *alleged* prostitute he was caught with. I'm sorry, but you need to top it or he will get the co-anchor position. I'd hate to do that when I know you are more than capable."

Sometimes Nola hated the news and wished they could call a cease-fire for the holidays. Life went on, wars continued, people died tragically and politicians cheated. She'd witnessed every sin imaginable and had even committed the ultimate one herself.

Shaking her head to erase the memory, Nola ended her call with Pete. She brushed her hair one last time and checked her reflection in the mirror before heading out. This was not the way Nola wanted to start her afternoon with Chase. Correction—with Kay and Chase. It wasn't a date and she shouldn't have to remind herself she was working. Besides, George was going to be there, and nothing was more unromantic than having a burly cameraman by her side.

The KWTT news van pulled up in front of her building. Normally she would've met George at the studio, but since her condo was on the way to the ranch, there was no sense in backtracking.

George was a friend Nola trusted completely. A veteran himself, George had witnessed more than his share of fighting and tragedy after serving twenty years in the Navy. Unlike Nola, he'd come to town to retire and wind down, not climb the ladder of success. George was one of the few people who knew of Nola's past and her current fears. Nola regarded him as a pinch-hitting father, and she was grateful George kept her secrets even though it must put a strain on his marriage.

"I see you dressed down today." George regarded her wardrobe choice and nodded. "I approve."

Nola looked down at her favorite buttery soft gray T-shirt, semi-faded jeans and cowboy boots. She was comfortable to a point but felt exposed without her Spanx. "I'm not sure how long I'm going to last in these boots. I bought them a couple years ago because everyone said I needed a pair in Texas, but I've hardly worn them. I'm going to get blisters."

George laughed at her. "You need to get out more and do some dancing to break them in."

"Why? To add blisters on top of my blisters? No, thanks. Besides, I don't dance."

"You need to learn," George said. "But have no fear. There's still a pair of your nasty old black Converse sneakers in the back of the van. At least I think that's what I smell."

"Why, you—" Nola hauled off and playfully smacked him. "That's not right and you know it. Stop laughing and keep your eyes on the road."

George composed himself and cleared his throat. "You and Chase looked pretty chummy at the baggage claim."

"Chummy? How?" Nola hoped she hadn't looked like a lovesick fan. Chase's hard, chiseled features had softened during the flight and Nola had begun to see a side of him she hadn't known existed.

Chase had always come across as the quiet, watchful brother in the background. During the Ride 'em High! and Dance of Hope grand opening, Nola had noticed how Chase allowed the rest of the family to revel in the spotlight, and Nola respected his modesty despite his exorbitant wealth.

The van stopped at a red light. "I do believe you're blushing." George lifted his sunglasses and leaned over the center console to take a better look. "You *are* blushing."

His encroachment on her personal space snapped Nola back to reality. "What are you doing?"

"Honey, you've got it bad." George whipped out his cell phone and snapped a picture of Nola.

"What was that for?"

"No one would ever believe me if I told them Nola West was not only frazzled, but frazzled over a man."

"You realize I know over a hundred ways to kill you, right?"

"Yeah, but you won't." George chuckled. "Besides you'll need me to be your bridesman at the wedding."

"Bridesman?"

"Who else is better suited to stand up for you when you marry Chase Langtry? You don't have any close friends nearby and you lean toward the unconventional. Instead of a bridesmaid, you'll have a bridesman. Me."

"You're deranged, you know that? I am not marrying Chase Langtry, or anyone else for that matter." Nola refused to allow herself even one second of imagining marriage to Chase Langtry. "We don't exactly run in the same social circles."

"Brace yourself, darlin'. We are about to enter Camelot."

Camelot was the nickname George and Nola had

given Bridle Dance the first day they'd seen the log home whose size rivaled that of a small castle. The horses lived better than Nola did. The familiar entrance to the ranch was majestic with its bronze rearing-horse sculptures on either side of the wrought iron sign. Only they'd never seen them with gigantic red bows around their necks. Nola was willing to bet that once the sun set, the main road would light up like a fairy-tale forest of sparkling lights.

The drive was unpaved and dusty, and Nola loved how the Langtrys had maintained a rustic atmosphere. With the exception of a few side businesses, like the winery and the sod farm, the majority of the ranch was devoted to horses.

"What on earth is that?" George asked.

"It looks like Santa." Nola peered through the windshield. "Are those real reindeer?"

"I hope not." George slowed the van as they passed the Christmas sleigh display. "They sure do look like it though, don't they?"

"That's borderline scary." Nola laughed. "I love Rudolph, though. Good God, look at the house. How many wreaths do you think they have on that thing?"

"Forget the house—there's your Prince Charming."

Chase waved from the garland-draped front porch, where boughs of holly framed the front door. As he stepped down the stairs, the sun glinted off his golden hair, and Nola thought it was unusual to see Chase hatless. There was nothing shading his gorgeous Caribbean blue eyes. Normally a man without a hat appeared more vulnerable to her, but the opposite held true with Chase. He looked more raw and rugged, and Nola was aching to run her fingers through his hair.

"Like I said, you've got it bad." George parked the van and smiled at her.

"If you do one thing to humiliate me, I promise you'll live to regret it." Nola watched Chase walk toward them and prayed she wouldn't embarrass herself.

Chase opened Nola's door before she reached for the handle. As he swung the door wide, a crisp breeze swept across Nola's face and chest. And that was when her body betrayed her. Victoria's Secret be damned, her nipples stood at attention right through her shirt.

A slow, easy grin spread across Chase's face. "You might want to grab a jacket if you have one. It's a bit chilly today."

So much for not embarrassing herself.

Chapter Three

Chase now had one more fantasy etched into his brain. He was sure Nola's reaction was due to the cool air and not his presence, but he could always dream. He noticed that Nola had heeded his advice and dressed down this afternoon. As distracting as he may have found her short skirt earlier, the way her jeans fit her backside was even more unsettling. She appeared slightly curvier and he liked it.

Chase made a mental note not to walk behind Nola for the remainder of her visit. He led his guests into the house by way of the great room, not realizing that neither one of them had ever been inside before until their gaped-mouth expressions told him otherwise.

Following their eyes three stories up toward a bevy of skylights, Chase gave them a brief history of the rustic home, hoping he didn't sound ostentatious.

"My father personally chose each log in this house, and every one came from the ranch's Western red cedar trees."

"It's beautiful craftsmanship." George admired the

monumental floor-to-ceiling river-rock fireplace. "It's a rarity to see this type of construction anymore."

"It was my father's vision. He had every log hand-hewn and notched on-site and wanted the house not only to be a one-of-a-kind structure, but also to be a home he could hand down through the ages to his children and eventually their children."

"How many of you live here?" George asked.

"Just my mother and myself nowadays." Chase looked around at the house that was once so filled with warmth. As much as he wanted to get married and start a family of his own, he couldn't help but wonder how his mother would feel staying in the massive home by herself with only Barney for company.

Langtry tradition had long dictated that when a child got married they moved into or built a house of their own on the property. With all of their land, they could live on the same ranch and literally be in the next county, but the idea had never appealed much to Chase. He wanted his children to grow up in the same house he had. He hadn't discussed it with any of his brothers, though, fearing it might set off an argument among them.

Jesse wouldn't care—he had his own ranch. But Cole and Shane might have a thing or two to say about him living in the main house when they had both chosen to refurbish midcentury cottages. Their father's estate had divided the ranch equally among the four of them, but the house remained solely his mother's. It was a moot point anyway—Chase didn't even have a girlfriend—but any decision about the house would ultimately be Kay's.

He turned to Nola and found her studying him as if she were trying to read his mind. It was unnerving, especially because she was the one who had triggered these it's-time-to-settle-down musings.

She quickly turned away and surveyed the room, her eyes landing on a large piece of artwork on the far wall leading to the kitchen. Chase moved to stand next to her but instantly regretted his decision when the enticing aroma of vanilla mixed with brown sugar greeted him. Chase had been around his sisters-in-law enough to be fairly sure that Nola shopped at Bath & Body Works.

"That was a gift from the local Native American Kickapoo tribe. It's my mother's favorite piece."

"I can understand why. It's breathtaking, but then again so is the rest of your house. Not quite what I imagined, though."

"What do you mean?" Chase asked.

"Log homes tend to be dark. This is amazingly light filled and warm at the same time. And I suppose I expected it to be as festive inside as it is outside."

"Trust me, it will be. Mom's planning a decorating party this weekend." For a split second, Chase envisioned Nola there beside him, hanging stockings on the mantel.

Nola lightly touched Chase's arm. "Your father created a lasting legacy. I wish I'd had the opportunity to know him."

"Thank you." That was all Chase could muster.

He liked the way she truly seemed to appreciate what his father had created, instead of carrying on over the grandness of the house, as many of his previous dates had—not that this was a date.

"Hello, Nola, George." Kay swept into the room and gave each of them a hearty hug. "I'm glad you could come out today."

"Thank you for having us. You have a lovely home," Nola said.

Kay tilted her head. "All these years and you've never been inside? Our door is always open to both of you, and George, any time you want to bring your kids by to go riding, please feel free."

"Thank you, ma'am," George said. "My wife and I would enjoy that."

Kay squeezed in between them and wrapped her arm around George, leading him to the kitchen. "None of that 'ma'am' nonsense. Kay is fine."

"Yes, ma—Kay," George sheepishly mumbled.

Nola smiled and turned to Chase. "I don't think I've ever seen him reduced to mush before. Remind me to thank your mother later."

"She meant what she said, you know." Chase reached for Nola's hand so George and Kay could walk ahead of them. The intimacy of the gesture surged through him, and for a moment, Chase questioned his own boldness. "You're welcome here anytime, and the invite is still open for you to join us for the Winter Festival and tree lighting."

"Thank you." Nola didn't attempt to move away. "I don't want you to think I'm ungrateful, but with my schedule—well, that's the problem. I don't really have a schedule. I'm an on-the-scene reporter and they call us at all hours. It makes it difficult to plan anything."

Chase hadn't considered that aspect of her job. He was used to traveling according to a set rodeo itinerary. Nothing was ever last minute. "It's not as though this isn't work related. Say yes, and if a bigger story comes up, I'll understand."

"How about we see how today goes, and take it from there?"

"Agreed." It wasn't the yes Chase had hoped for, but it was a step in the right direction. The more coverage the Mistletoe Rodeo gained, the more successful it would be. Although he had to admit, it would be much nicer to have Nola to himself, without George in the mix.

Facing each other, their hands still linked, Chase briefly forgot they weren't the only two people in the house. His first instinct was to kiss her. Right there in the middle of the great room, not caring who walked in on them. Everyone deserved to celebrate Christmas surrounded by love and family, and it bothered him that she'd probably spend hers alone in some tiny condo. That wasn't acceptable. Nola needed to experience a down-home Christmas, and he was determined to show it to her.

KISS ME, YOU FOOL. No, wait! Don't kiss me…not here anyway.

No one had ever thrown Nola this far off her game before. Bridle Dance was not Camelot, Chase was not

Prince Charming and she was far from a princess. *Get a grip, soldier.* Guys like Chase didn't fall for girls like Nola. She was way out of her league, and any thoughts otherwise would be a waste of time, leading only to disappointment. Nola didn't measure up to the Langtry women. She was a military brat with a tainted past and she definitely didn't belong in their world.

She released Chase's hand and followed him into the large but simple kitchen, which was perfect for entertaining a large family. Nola could easily envision the four brothers tearing through the house when they were children.

"I love the flooring in here." George squatted to run his hand over the wide planks and was greeted by a big, wet, black canine nose.

"Barney, behave. I'm sorry. He's a little enthusiastic around new people." Kay gently tugged on the dog's collar. "The floor is reclaimed lumber from the barns that used to stand on the property. Joe wanted to incorporate the old with the new, so the previous generations of craftsmanship have been woven into our home."

Nola reassuringly touched Kay's shoulder. "He succeeded beautifully." From previous interviews, she knew how difficult it had been for Kay, losing her husband to a sudden heart attack. There had been a deep love between Joe and Kay, one that had ended way before its time, taking their plans and dreams with it.

"Have a seat." Kay motioned to the counter stools

surrounding a large butcher-block island. "Chase said you were interested in covering the Mistletoe Rodeo and charity auction. My daughter-in-law Tess is adding the finishing touches to the website today. We're in a bit of a rush to get the news out there, since we plan to make this an annual event. Has Chase told you much about it?"

"We discussed it briefly over breakfast." Nola felt heat rise to her cheeks. It wasn't as if they'd spent the night together. Well, they had…but not in *that* way. "I'm ashamed to say today is the first I've heard of it."

"Is this your inaugural year?" George asked. "I haven't heard anything about it, either. What charity does it benefit?"

"The Ramblewood Food Bank, and yes, this will be the first year of many, we hope." Kay opened a folder and handed Nola and George information sheets. "With so many families in dire straits in this area, the need for a fully stocked food bank has arisen. We have a big event over Thanksgiving, which is wonderful, but as quickly as the food bank fills up, it empties. We want to raise enough funding with the rodeo and auction to keep the food bank replenished year-round, and we want to raise awareness so people continue to donate throughout the year, not just over the holidays. Poverty doesn't take a break."

Nola read over the statistics. "Look at the volume of inventory going in and out of the food bank in the course of one week alone—I had no idea it was this bad."

"Many people don't," Kay said. "I'm aiming to

make this an exciting yet educational full-day event. There will be a tricky tray auction in the morning, where you purchase a ticket and drop it into a fishbowl in front of the item you want to win, followed by a pancake brunch and then an afternoon filled with carnival-type games and an exhibition rodeo. The full-fledged auction will round out the event in the evening, where people can bid on everything from artwork to spa retreats. Various people and companies throughout the area have donated the items for both auctions, so one hundred percent of the proceeds will go directly to the food bank."

Multiple thoughts ran through Nola's head at once. It would be a great public interest story, especially because it focused on so many of the families affected by foreclosures and takeovers by corporate farms. Nola found it slightly ironic that the biggest ranch of them all—the very one who had purchased many of the smaller farms over the years—was the one hosting the event. Then again, it was better for the families to have made some profit selling their land to the Langtrys than to have lost everything to the bank.

"Do you think the food bank would be open to us shooting a segment there?" Nola asked.

"I think they'd love it." Kay clasped her hands. "I'm sure Chase would be happy to organize a meeting for you. He's my cochair."

Nola tried to figure out the look that passed between Kay and her son.

"Sure, I'll set something up this week," he agreed. *Did he wink at me? I think he did.* Chase Langtry was flirting with Nola and she liked it. Turning to address George, she noticed the wide I-told-you-so grin plastered across his face.

She nudged him with her foot. "Would you please run out to the van and get your camera?" Nola directed her attention back to Kay. "I had originally planned on shooting outside, but I think this setup works better. Would you mind repeating everything you just explained to us on camera? I'd really like this to be a multisegment story leading up to the day of the event."

"Really?" Kay asked. "I expected this to be a one-time thing. Thank you, Nola. The more people we reach the better."

After Nola wrapped the shoot, she found Chase on the front porch.

"I guess I owe you an interview of my own," Chase said when she approached. Thankfully, George hung back and gave them some distance. Nola hadn't been sure if Chase would hold up his end of the bargain.

"Only if you trust me." She took another step closer to him. Less than a foot separated them, and Nola fought the urge to lay her hand on his chest. "We can reshoot this as many times as we need until you feel comfortable. The van has full editing capabilities, so you'll see the final cut before I send it to the studio. But they are expecting something for the six o'clock news."

"No pressure, right?" Chase shuffled his feet and leaned on the railing. "Let's do this, then."

"I won't let you down," Nola said. "Just give me a chance."

Chase met her eyes as the words tumbled from her lips. She hadn't meant for them to come out so breathlessly. She'd meant to sound reassuring, not desperate.

CHASE SENSED THERE was more to Nola's statement. First Cole, then his mother had pointed out their mutual attraction. Up until this point, Chase had always assumed it was one-sided, but there was no denying the increasing chemistry between them. Chase wished George wasn't so close by so he could have a moment to show Nola how much he trusted her. There was never a more right and wrong time to kiss her.

"Where do you want to do this?" Nola asked.

Chase focused on Nola's mouth. Her lips were almost bare, just the way he liked them. She wasn't wearing nearly the amount of makeup she normally did, and her hair fell in natural waves instead of being flat ironed straight the way it usually was. This definitely wasn't Nola's customary in-front-of-the-camera attire and Chase wondered what type of interview he was in for.

"Are you able to walk and talk?" Nola asked, bringing Chase back to his senses.

Chase laughed. "Since I was a year-and-a-half old, yeah. I think I can handle it."

"That didn't come out quite right."

Chase rubbed the back of his neck and picked up the Stetson he had left on one of the rocking chairs earlier. "You make me nervous." It was an honest statement. One he feared left him a little too vulnerable where Nola was concerned.

Nola took his hand in hers and led him down the porch stairs toward the stables while George walked ahead of them with his camera, mumbling something about having to find their best light. Releasing Chase's hand, Nola instructed, "Relax, be natural and think of me as one of your friends." Only one problem with that statement. Chase didn't make a habit of holding hands with his friends, and in less than twenty-four hours, he had done so repeatedly with Nola.

Chase still felt her warmth in his palm. He understood it would be unprofessional for her to continue the gesture in front of her colleague, but he hated the immediate emptiness he felt when she let go.

"I know coming home without winning the championship was a big deal for you," Nola said as they continued to walk. "But going into the competition injured couldn't have been easy, either."

"No, it wasn't. But what was the alternative? I couldn't let everyone down. Do you know how many people put their time and money into my sponsorship? My friends and neighbors took time off work to travel to my events throughout the year. I had students cheering me on from the stands when I rode in their hometowns. Dropping out wasn't an option. I would've disappointed too many people. But in the end, I let them down anyway. I knew riding in the Nationals was a risk, but as painful as it was, I had to see it through. I never expected to be knocked

out of the competition on the second day, though."
Chase stopped walking and faced Nola. "It's different
around here. You're not just one person. You're part
of a community and they become a part of your family. When you travel for the rodeo, you get to know
your fellow riders' families, and even though they're
your competition, they truly become an extension of
yourself. Everywhere I looked, I had all these people
rooting for me. I had to ride."

Chase still physically ached from his final ride
in the ring, but explaining it to Nola had been easier
than he'd anticipated.

"Was your shoulder the only reason you were hesitant?"

Chase nodded. "At first I thought I had dislocated
it during a practice ride on one of our own broncs.
After a series of testing, the doctors discovered fine
tears in some of the ligaments. We took the physical therapy approach and I babied it the following
week. Even though I'd been warned that surgery
might be required down the road, I thought I was
strong enough to compete. It was still tender and I
knew the potential danger, but I didn't expect it to
end like this."

The corners of Nola's mouth turned upward
slightly. "No one can fault you for your dedication.
That's what you're known for."

Her declaration surprised him. "Thank you."

"Did you get that?" Nola glanced at George.

"Every word."

"Get what?" Chase looked from one to the other.

"You didn't even realize you were on camera." Nola squared her shoulders. Inhaling deeply, her smile broadened. "I don't think it needs much of an edit. Give us a few minutes to pull it up on the monitor and you can tell me what you think. If you hate it, we'll destroy it, but I think you'll be satisfied."

Chase watched them walk to the van, leaving him alone on the dirt path between the horse pastures. *What just happened?* Nola definitely had a way of interviewing people—if they even realized they were being interviewed.

He hoped he hadn't made a mistake by trusting her. Chase wasn't looking for anyone to validate his decision to ride in Vegas. He just wanted them to understand why he'd done it. More important, he wanted Nola to understand he still had something worth giving.

NOLA REALIZED SHE'D been taking a huge chance recording Chase without his knowledge. It was a plan she and George had come up with before they arrived at the ranch. They'd used the technique in the past, always granting the interviewee a chance to see the finished product. Most of the time it worked, but a handful of times it had gotten them in trouble.

Chase wouldn't have been as open if he'd known. And that was what he needed—raw honesty, so people could see this wasn't just another arrogant cowboy who'd blown his chances. Nola hoped Chase would feel the same way when he saw the video.

She was right. Very little editing was needed, and

even though Nola had done this a million times, she was nervous about showing Chase the result.

"Watch it all the way through before you say anything."

Chase stood outside the van and watched the monitor. His face remained stoic, and Nola couldn't get a read on what he was thinking. She even looked to George, but he only shrugged. When the video ended Chase still didn't say a word.

Nola tried not to be obvious about glancing at her watch. She had an hour left to get the video to the studio.

Chase jammed both hands into his front jean pockets. "Why did it look like I was about to cry?"

Bingo! That was exactly the effect she wanted. "Because this means something to you. It wasn't just about winning. It was about family and community—and not disappointing any of them. It shows who you really are, Chase. What do you think? Can we use it?"

Chase shook his head and turned to George. "Man's opinion, and be honest. Did it look okay or do I look like a total wuss who didn't get his way?"

"I think it looks like a man who believes he not only let himself down but everyone else, as well. I thought it was heartfelt, and my wife tells me I'm immune to those types of things."

Nola hoped Chase trusted their opinions. She may be cutthroat at times, but Nola would never put someone purposely at ease just to stab them in the back. She knew many journalists who did, and they were more successful because of it. It certainly was Dirk's

MO. Nola had more respect for people than that, and she believed you could produce a solid piece of news without sensationalizing it.

"Go for it." It was hard to read the emotion behind Chase's words and Nola wasn't sure if he was all right with the interview or just pacifying her.

Waving George off from sending the video, Nola held up her finger, signaling that she needed a minute alone with Chase.

She lightly ran her hand down Chase's arm, feeling his muscles flex beneath her touch. "Are you sure you're comfortable with this? Because if you're not we can try something else."

"You asked me to trust you, and I have confidence in your abilities."

Talk about pressure. Nola didn't have a crystal ball and she couldn't predict how people would perceive the video, but in her experience, this was a good reel.

"Chase, there are no guarantees in life and I can't promise this will go over the way I intend it to. I *think* it will, but public perception is a crapshoot."

"I have faith in you."

Within minutes, the final cut was on its way to the studio and Nola called the station to let them know. She was nervous about Pete's reaction, especially because this wasn't the piece he was expecting, but weaved in with the Mistletoe Rodeo lead, Nola hoped he'd be pleased.

"Usually my segment runs around six forty-five, give or take a few minutes, in case you want to watch it or let anyone else know it's on."

"I think I'll pass. I don't watch myself unless I've had a bad ride and need to figure out what to correct."

"Fair enough. I guess that wraps everything up here." Nola hesitated, hating to end the afternoon. "So I'll call you regarding the food bank—if you're still okay with arranging it."

"Are you two leaving already?" Kay walked toward the van. "Stay and have dinner with us. I have steaks and chicken marinating. We're grilling out tonight and I have more than enough food."

"I have to get home to my wife and kids," George said. "But Nola's free."

"Wonderful. I'll set another place at the table." Kay turned, heading to the house.

"Nothing like a good old-fashioned ambush to get your heart pumping." Chase laughed.

"George, you're my ride home," Nola said through clenched teeth. The nerve of that man to offer her up to the Langtrys. She'd figured he'd pull some sort of stunt, but in a way, she was secretly thrilled that he had.

"I'll take you home," Chase offered. "My way of returning the favor from this morning. But if you don't want to stay and would rather disappoint my mother, I perfectly understand."

Nola shook her head at George's all-too-obvious matchmaking. "Don't give me the puppy-dog look," Nola said to Chase. "I would be happy to join you for dinner."

As she reached into the van for her leather jacket

and handbag, Nola leaned over George's shoulder and whispered, "I'll get you for this."

"No, you won't... You'll thank me."

NOLA HAD BEEN around the Langtry clan numerous times over the years but never in so intimate a setting as a family meal. Chase's cousin Ella and husband, Nicolino, Bridle Dance's general operations manager, and their five children also joined them. Including herself, there were nineteen of them around the massive cedar table. Since they all lived on the ranch, this was the norm for them. It was loud, and at first Nola felt completely out of her element, but that quickly changed with everyone's welcoming manner.

In the background, though, Nola thought she noticed tension brewing between Chase and Shane. Almost as if Chase was avoiding his brother. She hoped her presence wasn't the reason.

After dinner, Nola helped clear the table despite Kay's protests that she was a guest. Later, she and Chase strolled through the pecan grove to work off an incredibly decadent chocolate cake Tess had made for dessert. Nola couldn't help but smile when she saw the trees glistening with thousands of twinkling white lights.

"Your mom must have some grocery bill." Nola hadn't sat at a table with so many people since she had last eaten in the mess hall.

"Mom doesn't know how to make small meals. It's only she and I in the house, but cooking just for the two of us goes against every fiber of her being.

If she didn't have everyone around, believe me when I say she'd be cooking for all the ranch hands. There are some nights she does that, too. Half of what she cooks comes from the garden. She cans in the fall, and the cellar has its own section filled with every kind of preserve imaginable. She donates quite a bit to the food bank."

Nola was aware Kay liked to give to the community, but there was more to the woman than most people realized, and her compassion needed to be celebrated.

"How would you feel about honoring your mom at the Mistletoe Rodeo to commemorate her hard work and commitment to the community?"

"I love the idea." For a moment, Nola thought Chase was going to kiss her and was slightly disappointed when he didn't. "I don't know why we didn't think of it before."

The temperature had dropped a solid twenty degrees since the sun had gone down and Nola pulled her jacket tighter across her chest.

"Are you cold?" Chase asked.

"Actually, I find it invigorating. I learned to adapt after the excruciatingly hot days in the desert. The cool nights were welcome, although sometimes they were downright frigid."

"I really do admire you for serving our country." He nudged her arm with his, causing her to look up at him. Tall in her own right, she normally rivaled most men in height, especially when she wore heels. Chase still had her beat by a good four or five inches.

Unable to maintain eye contact without blushing uncontrollably, Nola glanced down at the ground. The lights from the trees illuminated their path. "Thank you." Nola had never been comfortable talking about herself and wanted to change the subject. "What's going on between you and Shane? I hope it had nothing to do with my being there."

"Not at all. Shane is the person I let down the most when I lost. We haven't spoken since I arrived home because I'm not sure what to say."

"Tell him what you told me." Nola wanted to give Chase a comforting hug but feared she'd appear too brazen. "He's your brother and he loves you. I haven't seen my brother in eight years, but I don't doubt London's love for me and I'm sure he doesn't doubt mine."

"London, huh? Let me guess—that's where he was born?" Nola loved the dimples that appeared when Chase smiled.

"Conceived. We were souvenirs."

"I can't imagine going a month without seeing one of my brothers, let alone eight years. When was the last time you saw your parents?"

Nola sighed. "Three years." In her mind, it hadn't seemed that long ago, but when she said the words aloud, she realized she couldn't even remember the last time they'd spoken on the phone. "We were stationed on the same base in Germany for a few months. My family isn't sentimental the way yours is—I'm not saying that's a bad thing. As kids, we only saw my grandparents a handful of times. My parents never took the time to visit them. I'd love it if my mother and father would make the trip here, but that's very unlikely. A phone call here and there is enough for them. My brother's no different. I guess that's why I don't see Aunt Jean and Uncle Dan that often. It just wasn't something we grew up doing."

They'd arrived at a section of unlit trees, and Chase stopped and leaned his back against one of the massive pecans. The nearly full moon filtered through its limbs, casting playful shadows on the ground. Nola lifted her arms and made her own shadow dance among them. Chase snickered as he watched.

"What's so funny?" Nola leaned in and playfully pushed at his chest, but she was caught off-guard when he snaked his arms around her waist and tugged her flat against him.

"Mr. Langtry," Nola said in her best Scarlett O'Hara voice. "I do declare."

"I'm sorry, ma'am, but it's tradition," Chase replied with a pretty good Rhett Butler impression of his own.

"Tradition?"

"I believe I spotted some mistletoe in this here tree earlier today."

"Mistletoe?" Nola remained in character. "Above us, right now?"

"Why, surely, ma'am," Chase continued and Nola tried her best to keep from laughing. "'Tis the season and all. You wouldn't want to break a long-standing custom, now, would you?"

"No," Nola said. "I wouldn't want to do that."

Chase was only a hairbreadth away, and then he

moved even closer, his lips brushing hers. Afraid he'd pull away, Nola laced her fingers behind his neck and deepened their kiss. Her lips parted, inviting him in, not the least bit shy about having a taste of Chase for herself. Her hands slid down his chest and slowly worked their way around his waist and into his back pockets, inciting a low guttural growl from him. *And so much for not being brazen.*

Through the thin leather of her jacket, Chase's thumb grazed her breast. "You're driving me crazy," he whispered.

"Not half as crazy as you're making me." Nola closed her eyes and reveled in the warmth of his body while one random thought ran through her head. *Thank you, George.*

Chapter Four

Chase dropped Nola off at her condo a few hours later. While her body yearned to invite him in, the little angel sitting on her shoulder won the coin toss and Nola said goodbye at the door. Now she was kicking herself for the restraint.

She would've been able to handle Chase's departure better if he hadn't kissed her goodbye. Their first kiss under the moonlight in the sparkling pecan grove definitely won the prize for most magical, but this one had been more intimate and passionate, wrapping her in a euphoric cocoon.

Resting her head against the door, Nola resisted the temptation to peer through the peephole to see if Chase still lingered in the hallway. She turned, flattening her back against the doorjamb as her fingers skimmed over her lips—lips that still tingled from the memory of his mouth upon hers.

Curious to know how the public perceived Chase's interview, Nola dragged herself away from the doorway and headed to her computer. She checked the social media sites first, then the local stations. The impact was good, but it could've been better, at least in Nola's eyes.

The majority of people had sympathized with Chase rather than condemned their hometown hero. Then there were those who just resented the Langtrys in general and didn't hesitate to call them out. Nola compared her interview to ones shot moments before his Vegas ride. His nervousness had been virtually undetectable, which was surprising considering what she now knew about his injury. Years in the spotlight had seasoned Chase in hiding his emotions. Nola hoped that facade didn't carry over into his personal life, although she herself had been schooled in the art of hiding her true feelings when she was only a child. "Keep it to yourself," her father would command whenever she and her brother had shown any sign of *weakness*. Once someone knew how you felt, you were at their mercy.

One person repeatedly blasted the Langtrys in the comments section on multiple sites. Scott David. Nola recalled hearing the name before but couldn't quite place it. A quick search revealed he was a wealthy Texas cattle baron. Why would he hold such a strong grudge against the Langtrys? His comments weren't directed at Chase, per se; instead, they were aimed at his deceased father.

In all her coverage of the family over the years, Nola had never heard anyone speak harshly against Joe Langtry. He had been a tough yet fair businessman who had aided many fallen ranchers in the community by offering them above-market value for their land so they wouldn't go into foreclosure. Sometimes he had leased it back to them when they chose to stay in business. Other times he had absorbed the land into Bridle Dance, growing it to the size it was today.

Scott David wasn't specific in his jabs, but it was clear the man had an ax to grind. Then again, what was a handful of negative comments amid thousands of good ones?

Nola closed her laptop and dug through her bag for her phone. She hadn't checked her messages since George had left, and she prayed she hadn't missed a call from the station. Normally she didn't silence her ringer, but she hadn't wanted to offend her hosts by having it go off in the middle of the meal. Engrossed in the Langtry family revelry, she'd forgotten to turn it back on afterward.

There was one voice mail from Pete asking Nola to meet with him in the morning and two texts from George: Was I right? Followed by another, two hours later: Since I haven't heard back from you, I take that as a yes. Lunch is on you tomorrow.

Checking the time, Nola decided it wasn't too late to call George to see if he'd heard anything from the station.

The cameraman's deep chuckle resonated through the phone. "I can't decide if I want fish tacos from Jimmy's or vodka rigatoni from Clark's."

"You're that sure of yourself?" Nola knew enough not to play coy with George. He'd see right through her.

"You're not using your normal exasperated tone, so…yes, I am."

"Okay, you win, but don't expect me to kiss and tell, so—"

"You kissed him?" George fumbled with the phone. "Hey, Betty, she kissed him."

Nola heard George's wife in the background cheering at the news. She hadn't meant to give away their kiss, and normally she wouldn't have if Chase hadn't left her so flustered.

"You're not getting another thing out of me." Nola wanted to steer the conversation away from her love life, if you could call it that. "I got a voice mail from Pete telling me to meet with him tomorrow. Have you heard any rumblings on what it's about?"

"I stopped at the studio after I left the ranch. I know they liked the segment, but keep in mind, Nola, it's not what they asked for."

No, it wasn't. Nola knew she'd be up all night worrying about it.

"I won't keep you. I'll give you a call after my meeting tomorrow."

"I'm sure it's nothing big," George reassured her. "Pete probably wants to know the direction you're taking this story."

"I hope so. Have a good night."

"Sweet dreams. Not that I have to tell you that— I'm sure you'll be dreaming of Prince Charming."

"Hush up." Nola hung up the phone. George was half right. She would be thinking of Chase, but the inflection in Pete's voice had left her uneasy. She was grateful for her job and gave it her all, even when she was covering the local 4-H livestock competition.

Nola decided on a cup of chamomile tea to help calm her nerves. While she waited for the water to boil, she looked out over her combination kitchen, dining and living room. The stark walls in the long, narrow room were cold in comparison to the warmth of the Langtrys' home. Her small condo had always been her refuge at the end of the day, but tonight it felt more like a prison.

She vowed to call her cousin Kylie the next day to catch up, and maybe she'd even stop in and visit with her aunt and uncle in Ramblewood. She couldn't remember when they were last together. Maybe a year ago? Too long, considering they were the only family she had stateside. *Family* wasn't a word Nola thought of often, but it was fast becoming one she missed.

CHASE AWOKE THE following morning with Nola on his mind. He hadn't planned on kissing her when they went for their walk, but the thought of kissing her in general had entered his mind once—okay, maybe ten times—throughout the evening. His physical attraction to her was nothing new and his family had reiterated that fact after he arrived home from dropping Nola off. He hadn't expected everyone to still be there. Normally they would've dispersed and gone home by that time, especially when the kids had to be in school the next day.

Instead, they'd sat around analyzing not only every look Chase had given Nola over dinner, but also every look he'd *ever* given her. He'd discovered that their scrutiny of his relationship—or whatever you called it—with Nola had been taking place for a while now. Embarrassed by his transparency, Chase made certain not to mention their kiss…kisses. He'd at least like some part of their evening to remain private.

Chase had dated his share of women, but he wasn't even dating Nola. Not yet anyway. Kissing her last night may have been a fluke thing, and at this stage, he'd be wise not to invest too much into it. In the back of his mind, the thought of Nola's occupation was like a red flag waving in his direction.

She was too driven and focused to devote much time to anything other than her job, whereas Chase was in the opposite position, walking away from his lifelong career. That was something she would never do. She might be regretting their time together already.

Chase headed downstairs and hesitated when he saw his mother in the kitchen. He braced himself for an onslaught of questions about Nola.

"Good morning, dear." Kay cracked a couple of eggs into a bowl. "I'm fixing myself some scrambled eggs and bacon. Would you like any?"

If Chase was smart, he'd say no and make a mad dash for the stables. But his growling stomach made the decision for him. "That would be great, thank you."

"Any idea when you'll take Nola to the food bank?"

"No, I forgot to mention it again last night. I'll give her a call later to arrange something." Chase rolled his shoulders to relieve the tension, feeling an instant jolt of pain on one side. Swallowing hard, he attempted to ignore his discomfort. "I'd prefer to stay busy, so if there's anything extra you need me to handle for the Mistletoe Rodeo, just let me know and I'll take care of it."

"Aren't you teaching today?" His mother faced him, spatula in hand.

"I can't do much with my shoulder. I have a doctor's appointment this afternoon, so I'm taking it easy until I hear what he has to say. All I can really offer is support and guidance from the rails."

"Are you avoiding the rodeo school or your brother?"

Chase had anticipated the third degree from his mother this morning, only he'd thought it would be over Nola, not Shane. "I am not avoiding anyone or anything, Mom."

"Yes, you are." His mother dropped slices of bacon onto a hot iron skillet. "You didn't want to talk about what happened in Vegas and I left it alone. We all did. We're giving you that respect and moving on, but I don't want to see you avoid everything rodeo related. Do you think you'll be able to perform at the Mistletoe event?"

While there was some light competition planned for the Mistletoe Rodeo, Chase had arranged for the majority of it to be executed by the Junior Rodeo kids to showcase their talents. He had even added pig and ostrich races to the roster. The barrel racers would compete dressed as elves and the bullfighters would wear Santa suits instead of their regular clown garb. It definitely wouldn't be a typical competition, and Chase had no issue with being a part of it. He just hoped Nola had been right when she'd said the good it did for the community would shift attention away from him and his epic fail. Ramblewood had never had a hometown hero, and this year had been his chance.

"I'll be there. Stop worrying. I'm not shirking my duties. Quite the contrary." Chase decided to test his decision out on his mother before he spoke with Shane. "I've already discussed this with Cole and I wanted you to hear it from me first… As far as I'm concerned, my professional rodeo days are over."

Chase watched his mother still for a moment at the stove, then continue to cook breakfast without any response.

"Mom, did you hear what I said?"

"I heard you."

Kay remained silent, leaving Chase uncertain what to say next. He fixed them both a cup of coffee while Kay set their plates on the table.

"I really expected you to say something about this." Chase joined her, pushing his plate to the side.

"I'm weighing my words very carefully." Kay shook some salt and pepper over her eggs. "You'd think I'd be elated to hear that I no longer have to worry about any of my sons getting killed or seriously injured in another rodeo. But this doesn't sit well with me and I'm trying to figure out why."

"It's what you've always wanted," Chase mumbled before taking a sip of coffee.

"Oh, no, you don't." Kay waved a fork at him.

"Don't you put this on me. This is the first I've heard you say you were retiring. After what happened this week, I feel as if you've given up on yourself. And as much as I've always hated that blasted rodeo, that's not what I want for any of my children. If you love something, do it…no matter how difficult it becomes and how many times you might fail."

Chase winced at her choice of words. "I'm not giving up by choice, necessarily. The doctors have already told me I risk potentially injuring my shoulder to the point where I won't be able to pick up my children. That's huge, Mom. To not be able to hold my own child because I was too stubborn to walk away. What kind of man would that make me? All that aside, I was coming to this decision long before the National Finals. I really want to devote more time to the ranch and the school. I'd expected to make this decision after my win this year, but it didn't turn out that way. I've accepted it and I hope you will, too."

"Have you spoken to Shane?"

"Not yet, but I plan to this morning. I'm annoyed at myself for even worrying about that conversation. I know my winning and staying on the circuit helps business at the school, but Shane can't live his dreams through me. He made his decision to walk away and nobody gave him any grief. I'd appreciate the same consideration. This is my decision, not his." Chase stood, leaving his untouched plate on the table. "I'm sorry, Mom, but I'm just not hungry anymore."

He should have gone to Cancun.

Retiring was a major deal for him and a decision

he had struggled with since his father's death three and a half years earlier. Cole had immediately left the rodeo and devoted his full attention to running Bridle Dance. Chase admired his older brother for taking on the massive responsibility of a multimillion-dollar paint and cutting horse operation, but a part of him felt guilty, as well.

Their father's will had left each brother an equal percentage of Bridle Dance, yet Cole had done—and still did—the majority of the work while the rest of them had reaped the rewards. Jesse reinvested every penny of his share back into the ranch, living off the profits of his own smaller operation. Shane and Chase did a limited amount of work on the ranch itself, devoting the majority of their time to the rodeo school. Chase did even less when he was on the rodeo circuit.

His family had been through hell since Joe's death. Especially when Shane and Chase had battled Cole and Jesse for control of the ranch's finances. The rodeo school and hippotherapy center almost hadn't been built because of a war among brothers. Chase had been the deciding vote, and he'd almost lost Shane when he had sided against him. He had no desire to escalate the tensions between them ever again, but he feared his decision to quit the rodeo might do just that.

The rodeo had been a part of his life for as long as he could remember. It was the last common thread he'd had with his father, and now it was gone. He hoped to regain some connection to his father by dedicating more time to Bridle Dance. Shane would have to accept it.

"What about breakfast?" Kay asked.

"Feed it to Barney. The minute I leave, you're going to make him a plate anyway. This way you won't have to cook twice." Chase gave his mother a quick kiss on the cheek. "I'll touch base with you later after I speak with Nola."

"Give her my best." Kay reached out and stayed him with her hand. "Chase, I don't think any less of you for retiring. As a mother, I want to make sure you're doing it for the right reasons. I had to ask."

Chase gave her shoulder a quick squeeze, headed toward the back door and snatched his black Stetson off the hook on his way out. He clambered down the porch stairs and headed toward his restored red 1954 Chevy pickup. Despite his net worth, it was one of the few things he owned for himself, and it was his most prized possession, next to his horse, Bocephus. Chase had named him after his favorite country singer, Hank Williams, Jr., who'd been given the famous moniker by Hank's father.

Normally he'd take Bocephus for a ride to clear his head, but this morning his horse wouldn't cut it. He wanted Nola. He needed to hear her voice, and the food bank gave him an excuse to call. Driving toward town, Chase dialed her number. Disappointed when he heard her voice mail greeting, he stumbled over leaving a message.

"Hey, Nola, it's Chase…Chase Langtry. I was wondering, if you—uh—happened to be free, if you—you might want to meet and d-discuss the Ramblewood Food Bank. That's if you have the time."

Well, that was brilliant. Chase was well versed in public speaking. Between interviews, the rodeo school and the various clinics he conducted throughout the country, leaving a simple voice mail shouldn't have been difficult. And it probably wouldn't have been if the feel of Nola's body against his wasn't still ingrained in his brain. His morning had had a rocky start and he knew Nola's straightforwardness and sensibility would refocus his attention on the Mistletoe Rodeo.

Who was he kidding? He just wanted the chance to kiss her again.

"You wanted to see me?" Nola stood in Pete Devereaux's doorway.

Looking up from behind his desk, Pete motioned for Nola to take a seat in one of the chairs across from him. The man regarded her for a moment, removed his reading glasses, walked to the door and closed it. Returning, he perched on the edge of his desk, making Nola instantly uneasy with him towering over her.

"The Chase Langtry piece was good but not what I had expected. You definitely appealed to the softer side of our viewers, but it wasn't the angle we agreed on. We shelled out a substantial amount to fly you and George to Vegas to capture a story, regardless of which way it went. With the exception of George's footage inside the arena, the trip was a waste. We're a relatively small studio—we can't afford to send two people on location and not have a story to show for it. Your only saving grace on this was the inclusion of the Mistletoe Rodeo. It's your story, but I don't think you're doing yourself any favors spending time on a holiday piece. Let me assign this to one of our rookies and you can concentrate on something a little more substantial."

The thought of someone else covering the Mistletoe Rodeo caught her a bit off-guard. She'd handed stories off in the past, but she wasn't about to loosen her grip on this one.

"With all due respect, I think there's more to the Mistletoe Rodeo than what you're seeing on the surface. You have an entire community reaching out to the farmers and ranchers in need. I was stunned at the demand on the food bank, and last night I discovered most towns around here don't even have one of their own. I'll admit, at first I thought this was a puff piece. But the more I spoke with Kay Langtry, the more I was convinced this is newsworthy. I would be happy to show you the footage we didn't use last night—I think you'll see what I mean."

"Nola," Pete argued. "Listen, you're a strong journalist, but—"

Nola held up her hand and stood. "It's a solid story if you give it half a chance. And an important one for our community and nationwide. Please don't belittle my decision to cover it. You have the final say, but if I'm the strong journalist you say I am, then you need to trust my instincts."

"I'm not questioning your instincts." Pete straightened, trying to maintain his height advantage.

"Yes, you are." Nola took a step toward him. "We

broadcast to a farming community. In my opinion, a story about their needs and the ways others can help is an important message to get out there. I'm sorry it doesn't contain a scandal or a violent crime, but I'm not willing to hand it off. Besides, without me there is no story. The Langtrys won't want anyone else."

"They would take any reporter if it meant coverage for their cause," Pete said drily, retreating behind his desk. "Your naïveté surprises me. If you want to run with it, you have my approval. I don't doubt that you'll do a good job. I just don't know if it will be good enough to take you where you want to go."

Nola smoothed the front of her skirt and then clasped her hands in front of her. "If there's nothing else, I'd like to get back to work."

"I need you to cover a press conference at ten. HC General has enacted a policy banning Christmas carols and holiday decorations at the hospital, and there's quite an uproar brewing over there."

"A Christmas piece?" Nola bit back her sarcasm. "And Dirk would be where?"

Pete slanted her a gaze. "He's meeting with the prostitute Senator Waegle allegedly hired."

"And our rookie field reporters?" Tension crept up her spine, but Nola refused to allow Pete to see her annoyance at the assignment.

"It's a slow news day." Pete replaced his glasses and sat in his chair without looking up at Nola, irritating her further. "I can't justify calling one of them in when you're available."

"Thank you for your time." Nola squared her shoulders, turned toward the door and opened it.

"Have a good day," Pete said.

Nola's back stiffened for an instant. *This job is only one step to bigger and better things.* The mantra had served her well over the years, reminding her to remain calm and accept that every crap job brought her a little closer to the big time.

"You, too." Nola strode down the hallway to her closet-size office. She squeezed between her filing cabinet and desk and sank into her chair.

She removed her phone from her bag. Seeing a missed call and voice mail notification from Chase created a slight flutter in her stomach. Ignoring them for a moment, Nola typed out a text message to George, asking him to come to her office.

Inhaling slowly, she attempted to steel her nerves before listening to Chase's message. Logic told her it was probably about the Mistletoe Rodeo story, but a part of Nola feared it might be one of those I-regret-our-kiss calls.

Chastising herself for fretting like a lovesick teenager, Nola pressed Play on her phone. The nervousness in Chase's voice immediately made her smile. She checked her watch. He'd called a little more than half an hour ago, and the realization that she didn't have enough time to meet with him bummed her out a bit.

She dialed his number, her pulse quickening when he answered with his Texas drawl. "Good mornin'. How are you?"

"Good." That wasn't exactly true, but hearing the sound of his voice brightened her morning. "How are you?"

"Better now."

Chase's declaration surprised Nola. Certainly, he couldn't mean that talking to her made him feel better. He must have been referring to some problem at the ranch that they had straightened out.

"Is everything okay?" Nola asked.

"It will be."

That didn't give her much to go on. "I'd love to meet with you today, but I have a press conference to cover this morning. Are you free this afternoon?"

"I have an appointment, but I'm open after two o'clock," Chase said. "How about we meet at the food bank? Do you know where it is?"

The food bank. Right. Chase wasn't asking her out for personal reasons. Of course he wasn't—his voice mail had clearly stated what he wanted. But she was annoyed with how let down she felt. Maybe Pete was right about the naïveté he'd so delicately pointed out.

"I can look it up online. Two it is. I'll let you know if I get hung up for any reason."

"Great. I look forward to seeing you." His voice, thick and warm, made her limbs feel like Jell-O. Nola was safer when he was fumbling his words. "I had a great time last night."

Bam! There it was. The words she wanted to hear—the words she *shouldn't* want to hear—but, damn, they felt good. "So did I."

"All right, well, I'll see you a little later."

Nola hung up and stomped her feet in excitement.

"By the look on your face I think you owe me another thank-you. I might hold out for lobster dinner instead of lunch."

Nola's hand flew to her chest. "George! How long have you been standing there?"

"Long enough to know you were on the phone with lover boy," George teased. "Hot date?"

"Hardly, considering you're coming with me." Nola grabbed the duffel bag she toted to all her field assignments from the top of the filing cabinet. It was filled with hair and makeup products and allowed Nola to convert the passenger side of the van into a virtual mobile styling center. "We're going to meet him at the food bank this afternoon, but right now we have a press conference to cover."

"What happened this morning with Pete?" George asked as they walked to the parking lot.

"He basically told me a holiday piece wouldn't win me any promotions and wanted to hand the story off to a rookie."

"What are you going to do?"

"I told him it's my story and I intend to see it through. I think this is the perfect time to discuss the plight of the American farmer. Poverty levels are soaring. I did some research last night and I see exactly what Kay meant by people being generous over the holidays but then forgetting the problem still exists once the season's over. And it's not just here. This is a national issue."

In theory, the story had the potential strength to

secure the co-anchor position, especially with Kay at the helm of the cause. When the Langtrys spoke, people listened. Their wealth earned them that influence. Nola only hoped covering this story was worth the risk, because she had a lot to lose at this point, including her heart if she wasn't careful.

Chapter Five

Chase's doctor visit went better than he'd anticipated. He hadn't done any further damage to his shoulder, and rest, along with continued physical therapy, were his only prescriptions. He could live with that. The rodeo school was almost finished for the year and the next session wouldn't begin until the first week in February. As long as he didn't get on top of anything that bucked for the next two weeks, he should be able to ride in the Mistletoe Rodeo.

Thinking back to the weeks leading up to Las Vegas, Chase realized he had been in a negative mindset going into it. Retirement had been at the forefront of his mind along with stress over the pending announcement. Even without his injury, he'd never had a chance of winning with that attitude. He'd given that same counsel to many of his students over the years.

After Chase heard back from Nola, he made an appearance at the school and managed to do some coaching from the fence rails. Taking Cole's advice, Chase had opted not to call his agent until after the holidays, but he knew nothing would change before then. He would prefer to hold off telling Shane a little while longer as well, but he knew he'd have to do it as soon as his brother arrived home. Shane had flown out to Colorado that morning to represent the school at a two-day rodeo clinic.

Chase's relationship with Shane had come a long way. Shane had some turbulent times in his past: a short-lived marriage to a rodeo groupie he didn't love, a baby boy he'd thought was his but who'd been taken away by the real father, a son with Lexi who'd been given up for adoption long before Shane had even known he existed and the financial battle with his brothers. Chase had to give him credit for turning things around, but a part of him still didn't fully trust what his brother's reaction to his retirement would be. It was a conversation he needed to have in person, not over the phone.

Chase pulled up to the Ramblewood Food Bank a few minutes late. The sight of the KWTT news van in the parking lot disappointed him. He'd forgotten Nola would have George with her, although of course he would be there to film the story. Nola stepped out of the van as he approached—long, lean legs beneath a fitted purple skirt and matching jacket. Nude high-heeled pumps made her legs appear endless, and Chase struggled to maintain his focus on why they were there.

Standing face-to-face with Nola, Chase wasn't sure what to do. Hug her, give her a peck on the cheek, shake hands? After their intimacy the previous night, anything less than a kiss hello seemed inadequate. But they needed to maintain a professional appearance. Jamming his hands into his pockets seemed like the best option.

"Hi." Apparently, he was incapable of forming more than one syllable.

"Hi yourself." Nola smiled, dimples he'd never noticed before gracing either side of her mouth.

"Wow, you two are great conversationalists." George walked between them shaking his head. "Before you wear each other out, let's get to work."

A tinge of red crept into Nola's cheeks, a flush Chase found endearing. One he feared matched his own.

After introductions and a tour of the facility, Nola and George began filming. "I'm Nola West, reporting from the Ramblewood Food Bank. We have over three hundred families living on or below the poverty line in Ramblewood and the surrounding areas. While the community generously donates food and clothing over the holiday season, continued support is vital to these families throughout the year. In a few weeks, in collaboration with the Bridle Dance Ranch, Ramblewood will host their first annual Mistletoe Rodeo, with all proceeds going directly to the food bank. Many area businesses are donating time, services and items for people in need. If you'll follow me inside, we'll show you the inner workings of the organization. With me today is Evelyn Koch, the food bank director. Evelyn, thank you for having us today."

"You're more than welcome." Poor Evelyn, a long-time friend of Kay's, looked as if she'd drop from nervousness at any moment. The older woman did her best to speak slowly and clearly, but maybe a little too much so. "We started the food bank for people who had a crisis in the family or unexpected medical bills. Some were heading into foreclosure and unable to make ends meet. Providing them with free food and clothing allowed them to focus on making their mortgage payments so they wouldn't lose their homes. The popular misconception about food banks is that the people who use them are lazy and don't want to work. Many people we aid have employment but are still having trouble staying afloat. Some don't even require long-term assistance. If you lose your job or you're starting a new one and there's a gap before you receive your first paycheck, we're here to help."

"I have to say, when I came in here I expected to see only food," Nola continued. "Clothing was a surprise, but it makes sense. What completely caught me off-guard was the amount of infant products—diapers, formula, toys."

"It's not just adults who need our help." The mention of children seemed to give Evelyn some strength. "Children especially feel the effects of this economic slump. While many are on meal programs provided by their schools, those programs don't provide enough to feed them for the entire day, and certainly not on the weekends or on school breaks. Demand on the food bank increases in the summer, especially when employed parents have additional child-care expenses."

Evelyn led Nola and George through the facility, explaining the various sections for the viewers.

"I see you're building an addition," Nola said.

"We'll have our unveiling after the Mistletoe Rodeo." Chase enjoyed watching as Evelyn's excitement began to override her nervousness. "The addition will triple the size of the food bank. It houses an industrial kitchen and large dining area where we'll be able to prepare and serve meals and accommodate those seeking temporary shelter. It's being built entirely by volunteers, with local companies donating a hundred percent of the building materials. We couldn't be more thankful. We, in turn, plan to pay their generosity forward by doing whatever we can to help the community."

"Look at all the presents you have wrapped and ready to go." Nola indicated a multidenominational holiday area housing presorted boxes filled with gifts.

"We'll deliver those on Christmas and during Hanukkah. Thanks to some very generous donations, every family will receive some items from their children's wish lists, along with the essentials to prepare their holiday meals."

For a moment, Chase thought he saw Nola waver, but she recovered quickly. He wondered if some part of this story was getting to her, making her think of the unhappy Christmases she'd experienced growing up.

"Poverty affects not only Ramblewood and the neighboring communities, but also many places throughout the country," Nola addressed the camera. "We ask that you contribute in any way you can to the Ramblewood Food Bank, whether it's through financial contributions, food or clothing donations or by dropping off an unwrapped gift for a child in need. Many local businesses are accepting donations on the food bank's behalf—just look for the RFB logo in the window or check the Ramblewood Food Bank website, which features a list of locations throughout the county. Anything you can do to help support this center is greatly appreciated."

Chase felt like an absolute hypocrite as he listened to Nola interview various volunteers. Although he respected his mother's tireless efforts to give back to the community, the fact that so many of his neighbors were struggling when he had so much bothered him. His ranch animals lived in better homes than some people he knew. Chase wasn't ignorant of the resentment that existed toward the Langtrys for that very reason and he honestly couldn't blame anyone. He supposed that might in part be what drove his mother in the work she'd done since her husband's passing: the need for acceptance and the desire to show that the Langtry family as a whole wasn't as greedy as they sometimes appeared to be.

The amount of people living paycheck to paycheck stunned Chase. He knew many of his friends didn't have the money to do some of the things they wanted, a stark contrast to his own experience. Growing up, he and his brothers had never wanted for anything, and when it came to horses and the rodeo, Chase's father had spared no expense. But the Langtrys had been determined to instill good values in their children. The boys didn't receive expensive cars when they got their driver's licenses—their first vehicles were hand-me-down ranch pickups that had seen better days. And even though the family could afford to travel anywhere in the world, they had usually gone camping at Callicoon Lake, where they rented an extremely rustic cabin.

"This year we are able to provide Christmas trees to all families in need thanks to a generous donation from the Wilson Tree Farm," Evelyn added. "We've also put together programs that allow children to come in and make ornaments and presents for their families at no cost, allowing them to feel as though they're contributing to the holiday."

Nola faced the camera once again, describing the events scheduled for the day of the Mistletoe Rodeo, then took a few steps to stand beside Chase. "We have one of the chairpersons of the Mistletoe Rodeo here with us today, Chase Langtry."

Now was about the time Chase wanted to strangle Nola. He was completely unprepared for an interview, but he managed to get through it unscathed. When George finally put the camera down and Nola stopped waving the microphone in front of his face, he noticed his three sisters-in-law standing in the background and went over to greet them.

"Bravo." Lexi applauded while both Tess and Miranda wolf whistled at him, causing everyone in the food bank to look in his direction.

"I think Nola brings out the best in you." Miranda poked Chase in the ribs as he ducked out the door.

"Shh." Chase looked around for Nola. "Keep your voice down."

"Relax." Miranda waved a hand at him dismissively. "She's getting her gear packed up—she can't hear us."

"I don't care. I don't want anyone else to hear you, either."

"Come on." Tess squeezed in between him and Miranda, draping an arm over each of them. "Dish, oh, brother-in-law of ours. You like her, don't you?"

"What are you doing here anyway?" Chase unwrapped himself from Tess's clutches, only to find himself inches from Lexi's expectant gaze. "Don't you all have jobs?"

"We do," Lexi said. "And today one of those jobs is dropping stuff off at the food bank."

"Imagine our surprise when we found you here," Miranda said.

"Considering the fact that I called Mom and told her Nola and I were meeting here this afternoon, I'm sure you couldn't have been that surprised."

"Okay," Tess confessed. "We knew, and now we want details."

"How can three such beautiful women be so vicious?" Chase teased. He knew the brides of Bridle Dance wouldn't give him a moment's peace until he admitted he liked Nola, but he refused to give them the satisfaction. "Nola and I are just working together."

"Then, leave it to us to correct that." Lexi motioned for the other two women to follow her as she crossed the parking lot to Nola.

Chase might as well sign his own death warrant right now. It was bad enough he had his mother playing matchmaker, but now he had his brothers' wives adding to the mix. This could only mean one thing—they were about to embarrass him in some way. He was doomed.

If Chase had a shot with Nola, he didn't know which was more likely to end in disaster—trying to win her over on his own or leaving it up to the terrible trio.

"DON'T LOOK NOW, but we have company." George nodded toward the group of Langtry women fast approaching.

Nola wasn't sure what to expect, but based on their welcoming attitudes the previous night, she didn't feel she had anything to fear, at least not yet anyway.

"Hey, Nola, George," Lexi said. "Thank you so much for taking the time to cover such an important story. I can't even begin to tell you how much this means to Kay and the rest of the family."

"You don't have to thank me. I'm embarrassed that I haven't covered this before. I knew of the food bank but I didn't realize how substantial a role it played in the community. I'm overwhelmed by the need for it."

"Are you willing to do a little more to help out?" Tess asked.

"Of course. What do you need?"

"Between the Mistletoe Rodeo and the food bank, we have thousands of cookies we need to make and decorate," Tess continued. "A bunch of us are meeting at The Magpie tonight for a baking party. My mom is lending us the use of the upstairs catering kitchen and we'd love to have you join us. We could really use the extra set of hands."

"Um, sure." Nola had to suppress the jolt of excitement that buzzed through her at the invitation. She couldn't remember ever being a part of something like it before. "I was going to stop in and see Kylie this evening—would it be possible for her to come along?"

"Of course, and maybe she can wrangle that boyfriend of hers into coming, as well. All of the Langtry men will be there, plus a few others."

"They will?" Miranda asked.

"Of course they will. Don't you remember?" A look passed between Lexi and Miranda that told Nola no such plans had been discussed with any of the men.

"Oh, yes." Miranda feigned innocence. "It must've slipped my mind."

"All right, guys. You can cut the act. I'll be there."

"Great," Lexi said. "Around seven tonight?"

"Seven, it is," Nola said.

"Have you lost your mind?" George said as the women walked away. "You don't know the first thing about baking. In fact, I don't even think you know how to turn on an oven."

"That's not true."

"You forget I've been to your condo. The only food you have in there is those frozen TV-dinner things."

"I know how to turn the oven on, George." Nola rolled her eyes. "I've just never had the motivation to do so."

"Well, I'll call the fire department and tell them to be on standby, just in case."

Nola punched George in the arm, hard.

"Ouch." George rubbed his biceps. "That hurt."

"Be glad that's all I did to you." Nola tugged at the bottom of her jacket. "I can handle making cookies. I can handle anything."

Nola hoped she could handle being around Chase so publicly again, because she was already having a difficult time controlling herself when all she wanted to do was kiss him.

A FEW HOURS LATER, Nola parked in front of The Magpie. Kylie hadn't stopped talking the entire ride over and Nola's brain could no longer keep up.

"Don't you just love this place?" Kylie's Texas drawl was thick with sugary sweetness. "I just adore the way Maggie has it decorated. Look at the front window. Even the magpie cutouts have little Santa hats on."

Tess greeted them at the door, pushing Santa Claus hats down low on each of their heads.

"'Tis the season." Tess beamed. "Everyone's upstairs. The men haven't arrived yet, but my husband tells me they should be here shortly. Kylie, isn't Aaron coming?"

"He said he had something to do beforehand. I hope he shows up."

Kylie and Aaron had stopped by Nola's condo a few times over the years, and Nola always had the impression that Kylie was much more into him than he was into her. It had probably been a good eight months since she'd last seen them together so she wasn't certain where the relationship stood, but based on the subject of her cousin's endless chatter this evening, she was ready to settle down and get married.

Upstairs, Kylie dragged Nola toward Miranda and a woman she'd seen over the years but had never met. "Nola, I'd like you to meet the baby I helped deliver a few years ago."

"You helped deliver?" Miranda laughed. "If memory serves me correctly, you stood in the corner shrieking while I caught that baby on the way out."

Kylie shot Miranda a look she had intended to be evil, only Kylie didn't have a mean bone in her body. "Anyway, this is Vicki Slater, Ella's sister-in-law. You know Ella from Bridle Dance, right?" Kylie didn't wait for Nola to respond before crouching down. "And this is her daughter, little Randi Lynn."

"I'm not little. I'm three and a half." She was a miniature version of her mother, all blond hair and blue eyes.

"It's nice to meet you, Randi Lynn." Nola held out her hand and the girl shook it enthusiastically. "And it's a pleasure to meet you, Vicki. I know I've seen you at various events, but we've never had a chance to talk. I had dinner with your sister-in-law last night at the Langtrys'."

"I heard." Vicki leaned closer. "I also heard Chase has a bit of a thing for you. Good for you. It's about time someone took that man off the market."

Off the market! Nola felt her stomach drop.

"You'd better not go off and get married before I do." Kylie stood with her hands on her hips. "I'll be furious."

"Oh, jeez." Miranda wrapped a protective arm around Nola's shoulders and steered her toward another crowd of women. "Don't pay any attention to them. It's a small town and rumors spread like wildfire."

Another round of introductions just about wore Nola out. She hadn't expected there to be so many people, and this was only half of them. She was even more surprised when her aunt and uncle arrived to partake in the fun.

Looking around the room, she was glad she'd taken the time to change into a pair of jeans and a vintage long-sleeved blouse. The suit she'd had on earlier was far too dressy for holiday baking with the girls.

Now, this was something Nola never thought she'd do in a million years. *Holiday baking with the girls.* The thought may not flow naturally in her brain, but she felt relaxed around everyone, especially when they stopped the marriage talk and began singing horribly off-key Christmas carols. Between bursts of laughter and botched lyrics, Nola didn't think a single song had survived unscathed.

After their first round of cookies went into the industrial ovens, the men finally appeared, Aaron included, looking as though they may have had a drink or two before their arrival. All of them, walking in with their arms draped around each other's shoulders, had very peculiar grins plastered across their faces.

Chase walked over to Nola and unabashedly gave her a kiss on the cheek. She looked around to see if anyone had noticed the kiss only to find Kay watching them from across the room. With a wink and a smile, she appeared to give her approval.

"What are you guys up to?" Nola asked, playfully pulling away from him.

"Me? I'm up to nothing. I am innocent in all of this." Chase removed his Stetson and replaced it with a green elf hat complete with a bell on the end.

"All of this?" Now Nola definitely knew something was going on.

She turned to the sound of a pair of hands clapping loudly behind them. Maggie Dalton was trying to get the men's attention so she could put them to work.

"I think you guys need to do something that doesn't involve frosting. By the looks of things, you're already a little frosted. Tonight you're going to learn how to make red and green fortune cookies."

Nola had to hand it to the Langtry women. The way almost everyone was paired up, she wondered if she was on Noah's ark. Amazingly enough, the men didn't seem to mind too much that they were there. Although their cookies lacked some aesthetic appeal, the few she tasted were pretty good. The best part was making them alongside Chase, who was determined to out-bake her even though she'd had a head start.

"Okay, ladies." Maggie once again attempted to gain some semblance of control. "For anyone who doesn't know how to flood a cookie with royal icing, come over here and I will show you how to decorate the perfect sugary creation."

Between her four cups of hot chocolate and all the confectioners sugar, food coloring and festive sprinkles, Nola had a feeling she would look and smell like a Christmas cookie long after New Year's Day. By the time they had finished, all the freestanding racks were filled.

"I think we should have a taste test," Aaron announced once they'd cleaned up the kitchen. "Men against the women. Starting with my cookie versus Kylie's."

"I think that's a wonderful idea," Maggie said. "Why don't you each choose one for the other to taste?"

"We're judging each other's cookies?" Kylie asked. "Piece of cake. Mine wins."

"That's not fair." Aaron pouted in jest. "You haven't even tasted mine yet."

Nola felt Chase's hand touch the small of her back, guiding her in Kylie's direction. She noticed he had his cell phone in hand, then realized the rest of the men did, as well. Silently questioning Chase, she received only a chin nod toward Aaron and Kylie in response.

"Taste mine first." Kylie handed Aaron an elaborately decorated chocolate reindeer with nuts and coconut resembling fur. "Then you'll see what true cookie perfection is."

Aaron took a bite, nodding as he chewed. "This is good. This is really good. But I'm not quite sure it stands up to mine."

Aaron handed Kylie a red fortune cookie with white-chocolate-dipped ends. "Try it."

Kylie picked it up and turned it over, trying to hide her "it's a fortune cookie how good can it be" face. She cracked it open, and a diamond ring dropped onto the stainless-steel counter. A collective gasp echoed throughout the room while the men all held up their cell phones, taking photos and video.

Aaron retrieved the ring and held it in front of him. "I know I haven't been the easiest man to put up with for the past three years. I had planned on asking you this on Christmas Day, but with Maggie's help I decided to do it tonight, in front of all of our friends and family."

Aaron knelt on one knee, taking her hand in his, and slid the ring onto her finger. "Kylie West, will you do me the honor of becoming my wife?"

Kylie jumped up and down, almost knocking Aaron over, screaming, "Yes! Yes, I'll marry you!"

Nola looked at Chase. "You knew about this all along, didn't you? That's why you guys all came in together, after a celebratory drink."

"More like a drink of courage for Aaron. And yes, I knew he was going to propose to your cousin tonight." Chase laughed. "The only other people who knew were your aunt Jean and Maggie."

Before Nola could congratulate her cousin, Kylie pulled her into a suffocating hug. "Promise me you'll be my maid of honor."

"What?" Nola pushed Kylie's big hair and Santa hat out of the way so she could breathe.

"My maid of honor." Kylie held her at arm's length. "You have to say yes. There's no one else I would want."

"But what about your friends?" At the same time, Nola overheard Aaron asking Miranda's husband, Jesse, to be his best man.

"They'll be my bridesmaids, just like I was at their weddings. This honor is reserved for family."

"Okay, yes. I'd love to."

Kylie gave her another squeeze. Nola had to tame her own excitement. Not only was she surprised her cousin had asked, but it was also the first time she'd ever been in a wedding party, and that thought alone thrilled her. Too bad Chase wouldn't be the best man because she would love to walk down the aisle with him.

Where the heck did that come from? One night with a room full of giggling females and she had already succumbed to wedding fever. Without warning, an unwelcome thought pushed its way into her consciousness: no matter how much she enjoyed spending time with Chase, his family and his friends, once they learned the truth about her, they may not want her around anymore.

Chapter Six

With the rodeo school and taking Nola around to interview various people for the Mistletoe Rodeo, Chase had successfully kept his mind off his Vegas loss. The more time he spent with Nola, the more attracted he became to the woman she was, and not just the smoking body that had originally caught his attention.

Chase had accompanied Nola and George on a few live-coverage news stories. Her composure was constantly resolute, even when they arrived on the scene of an accident along the interstate before the paramedics. Nola's willingness to jump in and help the victims, not caring if she ruined her clothes in the process, had surprised him, although it shouldn't have knowing her military background.

George had remarked on her preparedness for any situation, explaining how Nola kept the back of the news van stocked with trauma-related items in case she needed them. Even though it wasn't part of her job description to do anything other than report the news, George said that on many occasions he'd taken over as reporter and videographer while Nola lent a helping hand.

Now Chase was supervising his students as they completed their required morning workout in the on-site fitness center. Training at Ride 'em High! included a comprehensive regimen that helped build the muscles a competitor needed to succeed in the arena.

His shoulder felt better this morning, making him want to climb onto the back of a one-ton bull and ride out his frustrations. But as much as he'd love to demonstrate dismount techniques today, Chase knew the risk was too great and had handed control of the class off to one of his instructors.

"Happy birthday, bro." Cole slapped Chase on the back.

"Don't remind me," Chase grumbled. Turning thirty wasn't all it was cracked up to be, especially when facing retirement with a body that had seen more injuries than most people experienced in a lifetime. Thirty may not sound old, but it certainly felt it lately.

"Don't go getting all girly on me and pulling this I'm-over-the-hill crap, because I have five and a half years on you and I can still kick your butt. It's just a number."

"You're married with a seven-year-old daughter. You and Tess are actively trying to have another kid. Jesse and Shane have their families, too. Not for nothing, I'm a little jealous of what you have."

After Chase dismissed his students so they could

clean up and grab breakfast, he and his brother started walking to the main house.

"You make it sound as if you're a troll living under a bridge," Cole said. "You have plenty of time. None of us were married at your age."

"Maybe you weren't, old man." Chase elbowed his brother. "But Jesse and Shane were close enough."

"You're just starting a relationship with Nola, whether you want to admit it to all of us or not. Give it some time to grow and see where it goes."

"I don't really see things with Nola going anywhere. You've heard her talk. She's made it clear that KWTT is just a stop along the way. She's not going to quit until she's sitting behind the anchor desk of one of the large news networks. Say this did work out—I can't ask Nola to give up her dreams to live in a little Podunk town. I wouldn't have given up my dreams for anyone, so why should I expect her to?"

"Because dreams change," Cole said. "You're a prime example of it."

"No, I'm not." Chase's frustration grew. "That's what you and Mom don't understand. It was never my dream, it was Shane's, and now I want more involvement on the Bridle Dance side of things. Would this have been the year I retired if it weren't for my injury? Probably, but I'll never know for sure."

"Okay." Cole held up his hands in defeat. "But I think you should tell Shane when he gets in before Mom lets it slip. Enough about that for now. It's your birthday. Jesse, Shane and I want to take you out tonight to cut loose a bit and have some fun."

Chase swallowed hard. "I didn't think Shane was flying home until tomorrow."

"He was able to catch an earlier flight." Cole stopped at the fence behind the house. "I have to head back to the office. What do you say about tonight?"

"Sure, sounds great." Chase unlatched the gate and a big black canine nose greeted him in the crotch. "Easy, Barney. I'd like to have the opportunity to have children before you castrate me."

Chase hadn't told Nola it was his birthday, but it didn't seem like much of a celebration without inviting her. Not that he felt like celebrating.

Christmas music immediately assaulted him when he entered the house through the back door. As far as he knew, his mother wasn't even home. She was usually bustling elsewhere about the ranch somewhere by now. He didn't really mind the music, though. The first year after his father's death, his mother had had zero interest in Christmas. It wasn't until Cole and Tess adopted their daughter, Ever, that Kay had begun to celebrate the holiday again. With the addition of his other nephews, Christmas became what it once was in the Langtry household: a celebration of family.

Chase wondered how Nola felt about children. Judging by the way she interacted with the kids on the ranch, he assumed she'd one day want her own. Wasn't that what all women wanted?

He removed his phone from his pocket and called her.

"Hey, I can only talk for a minute because I have

meetings all day and two assignments tonight," she answered briskly.

Nola's immediate dismissal, before he'd even said hello, crushed Chase's spirits.

"And here I was going to invite you out tonight."

Chase noted Nola's hesitation on the other end of the line. "I can't promise anything, but if I wrap up these interviews early, I'll give you a call. Where did you have in mind?"

Had he misread the situation between them? The lack of enthusiasm in her tone made Chase wish he hadn't bothered calling.

"Slater's Mill. My brothers and I are going, and if you can make it that would be great. I won't keep you from your work." Chase ended the call and turned his attention to making himself a cup of coffee. Spinning the K-cup dispenser, he found several flavored coffees—peppermint, eggnog and cinnamon—along with a variety of hot chocolates. Not a single regular dark roast in the house.

Chase enjoyed a flavored coffee every now and then, but a man needed a strong brew in the morning. He was willing to bet his mother had stocked his students' coffeemaker with the same flavors.

Chase had a little over an hour before he needed to be back at the rodeo school. It was enough time to run into town and get a real cup of joe. He went to grab his keys off the hook by the back door, but they weren't there. Neither were any of the other keys. Chase walked outside and checked the side parking area where they normally kept their vehicles, and with the exception of his truck, every one of them was gone. Including his mother's Mercedes, which rarely went anywhere.

Chase quickly dialed Cole. "Okay, what's going on?"

"What are you talking about?" Cole asked.

"My keys—all the keys to every vehicle—are gone. There isn't a single car here. I can't drive to The Magpie to get a cup of coffee without some form of transportation."

"Isn't there coffee in the house?"

He paced the kitchen floor. "Cole, where are my keys?"

"How the hell would I know? I don't drive your truck. You never let anyone touch it. I'm surprised you even allow Nola to ride in it."

"Then, where is everyone else?" Chase demanded.

"I saw Mom head out early this morning. Shane's Jeep is at the airport, two of the Navigators went in for service and I loaned Nicolino the other one because his truck broke down this morning. Sorry, Chase, but you're either going to have to find your keys or ride Bocephus into town. Hate to cut you short, but I need to get going."

Cole hung up before Chase could argue. He searched the whole house for his keys, even checking the ignition of his truck in case he'd left them there. It was his own fault for not having a duplicate set made. It had been on his to-do list for years and he'd never gotten around to it. So much for that cup of real coffee. Back inside, Chase popped an eggnog-flavored K-cup into the Keurig.

"Happy birthday to me."

"I HATED LYING to him like that." Nola looked up at Miranda, Lexi and Tess, standing shoulder to shoulder on the other side of her desk.

"Trust us—by the end of the night he'll be feeling much better. Especially with you by his side."

Nola still couldn't believe the "brides of Bridle Dance," as Chase affectionately called them, had shown up at her office first thing this morning and asked her to be a part of Chase's surprise party. She'd had no idea it was even his birthday, a fact she wondered if he had intentionally left out.

"Are you sure he wants me there?" The little voice in Nola's head told her Chase hadn't mentioned it for a reason.

All three women laughed—some might even say cackled—in unison. It was cute but becoming somewhat frightening. The interest they'd taken in Nola's relationship with Chase was a tad intense at times and Nola wasn't sure whether to believe they were telling the truth, or whether it was all just wishful thinking on their part.

"He just called and asked you out for tonight," Tess said. "I'd take that as a definitive yes."

Nola had enjoyed the time she'd shared with Chase over the past few days, but they'd spent the majority of it working. They'd never actually been out on a date or spent any time alone other than that first night, although she assumed that was what Chase had been attempting to do today.

"Should I get him anything?" Nola mentally ran through what she knew about Chase, and his only hobby seemed to be his truck. Anything rodeo related was a sore subject right now.

"Nope." Lexi shook her head. "Just bring yourself."

"Hopefully I won't let anything slip today. I had planned to discuss some ideas with Chase about honoring your mother-in-law at the Mistletoe Rodeo. If you have any thoughts on the ceremony, please let me know."

"We love how you came up with that idea, but don't overdo it." Tess stopped herself and winced. "That probably wasn't the best choice of words. I just mean Kay doesn't like attention drawn to her, so where a mention would be fine, an outright ceremony would probably embarrass her."

"Tess is right," Lexi added. "I think anything that detracts from the event and what she's trying to do with the food bank awareness campaign might actually upset her. We know you mean well, and it doesn't surprise me that Chase wants to put Kay in the spotlight to acknowledge all she's done for Ramblewood. I personally feel this is one of those things that would probably be better if it was held among her family and friends. Not a public event."

"I hadn't thought of that." There were people out there who'd probably accuse the Langtrys of organizing the fund-raiser just for the recognition. Namely

Scott David, who had increased his online ranting. Nola had yet to discover the basis of his resentment toward them, but his cutting remarks became more personal with every post. "I'll talk to Chase about making it a private affair. You're absolutely right."

"Thank you for understanding," Lexi said. "And don't worry about it tonight—you'll have the entire weekend with Chase at the Winter Festival to discuss the Mistletoe Rodeo."

"I will?" Chase had asked her to go, but she'd put it out of her mind and had no formal plans to attend. Plus she was on standby for the station, so it wasn't as if she could promise anyone she'd be anywhere.

"Kay asked us to invite you to our tree-trimming party tomorrow night." Miranda shifted, nearly causing an avalanche of files to tumble off the credenza behind her. "It's tradition. We begin at the town square and watch the Ramblewood tree lighting together, then we head back to the ranch and decorate the inside of the house from top to bottom. It will be so much fun. Please say you'll join us."

"Um, I don't know about that." Chase had mentioned her covering the festival and tree lighting, but he'd never so much as hinted about going back to the ranch. "That's your thing with your family. I appreciate you asking me, though." Nola could envision what the Langtrys' house must look like with everyone decorating together. "If a story breaks—"

"If a story breaks, you'll leave. At least give us a chance."

Nola almost laughed aloud at Lexi's words. Here

she thought they were giving her a chance when they thought it was the other way around.

"I'll talk to Chase tonight and see if he wants me there." Nola tried to figure out how she'd weave that into the conversation.

"I'm positive he'll ask you before you even have the opportunity." Tess smiled confidently. "And if he doesn't, we'll leave the decision up to you."

"Nola, I—" George hesitated in the doorway. "Hey, ladies. I'm sorry. I didn't mean to interrupt."

George's timing was perfect. "No, it's fine," Nola assured him before turning her attention back to her visitors. "I promise to be there tonight, and the rest we'll play by ear. I hate to run off, but George and I have a meeting to attend. I'll catch up with all of you later."

Nola stood, suddenly realizing how tightly packed her office was with four additional people in it. She'd never considered herself claustrophobic before, but the Langtry presence could be a bit overwhelming at times.

After the women left, Nola flopped into her chair. "It's not even eight o'clock and I'm already exhausted."

"Do you ever feel as if you're a fly caught in a web?" George chuckled.

"They mean well and I'm probably more sensitive to it because I'm not used to having family around. To them it's normal—to me it can be a little stifling. The Langtrys are good people and I enjoy spending time with them." Nola hoped it continued after the Mistletoe Rodeo was over and they had their news coverage. They'd never given her any reason to doubt their feelings were genuine, but Nola's insecurities drove her to mistrust the people closest to her. Except for her aunt, uncle and cousin, and that was only because they didn't know the truth.

Nola was relieved when the end of the workday rolled around. She had had to wrap up her interviews and editing early for Chase's party, and they had covered an emergency town council meeting on the other side of the county about the excessive numbers of Santa Clauses roaming the streets. One even had a deer on a leash.

It seemed to Nola that the more people tried to celebrate the holiday, the more people wanted to squash it. She'd thought the hospital's ban on all things Christmas was bad enough; now some wanted to make it illegal to dress as Santa. Honestly, she was surprised they hadn't added an elf clause to their new law. They could stand to learn a thing or two from Ramblewood's festive spirit.

With not enough time to run home and change before the party, Nola dug through the spare clothing options she kept on hand in her office. A person could never be too prepared. Nola never knew from one minute to the next what story she might have to cover, so whether it was a turkey pardon on Thanksgiving or a black-tie affair at the art museum, she had a standby outfit ready to go. She'd never been to Slater's Mill before, but from what she could find online about the honky-tonk, jeans and a flowing bohemian top with a pair of strappy sandals should work nicely.

She pinned the top sections of her hair back loosely and double-checked her reflection in the full-length mirror on the back of her office door.

Nola arrived at the bar only moments before Chase and huddled in the dark with the Langtrys and half the town. A sliver of light appeared as Chase opened the door.

"Why is it so dark in here?"

"Surprise!" everyone shouted as the lights came on.

Nola saw Chase stumble backward, almost knocking Jesse over. When he recovered from the shock, he punched each of his brothers in the arm.

The entire Langtry family, children and all, pushed their way toward the front of the room, ushering Nola along with them. Seeing her in the crowd, Chase smiled and reached for her. Grabbing his hand, Nola was surprised when he tugged her into his arms and kissed her in front of his family and friends.

"Wow," Nola breathlessly said. "Happy birthday."

"I'm glad you're here."

"Me, too." This time it was her turn to kiss Chase, and she did, long and hard, not caring who was watching. The sound of laughter and applause around them intensified as Chase drew her tighter to him.

Throughout the remainder of the evening, Nola stood at Chase's side, his arm firmly wrapped around her waist and his fingers locked into one of her belt loops. Nola watched people's expressions as he introduced her to them. No one seemed surprised or off-put that she was with Chase. They hadn't defined their relationship, but if this didn't feel like dating, she didn't know what did.

Tucked against him, she reveled in the way he casually glanced at her and the soft kisses he periodically placed on her cheek for no reason whatsoever. She was actually Prince Charming's date for the evening. After watching him from afar for so long, the moment felt surreal. And when Kay invited her along with the rest of the family to come back to the ranch for coffee, it felt natural to say yes…as if she actually belonged.

Back at the ranch, Kay brought out stacks of photo albums showing Chase throughout the years. He seemed a tad embarrassed, but Nola thought it was sweet. She was fairly certain her parents didn't have any photo albums of her. She had a few loose snapshots taken over the years, but none of them contained her entire family together.

"I can sense a kindred spirit from a mile away." Miranda settled in beside her on the couch. "You don't have much family, either, do you?"

From the little Nola knew about Miranda Archer-Langtry, she had zero family to speak of.

"My parents are stationed in Europe, and so is my brother. We were never one of those close families. Certainly not like this."

"It's a lot to get used to, but you'd be surprised how easy it becomes." Miranda acknowledged her husband across the room with a slight raise of her chin. "Joe Langtry died shortly after I came to town. Unfortunately, I never had the opportunity to meet him.

And even in the midst of this family's grief, they welcomed me in as if I'd been one of their own all along."

While Nola listened to Miranda, she noticed a man she'd never seen before walking into the room.

"Who's that?" Nola asked.

"That depends on who you ask. Jon Reese is the family's personal attorney, but he's also my best friend from Washington, DC." Miranda waved to him but she didn't catch his attention. "Jon grew up here in Ramblewood. He's actually the one who pointed me in this direction. Long story short, I took a gamble by moving here and won an amazing family. I'm surprised Jon wasn't at Slater's Mill earlier."

"He looks so serious...as if someone died," Nola whispered. She noted the grim expressions the four brothers exchanged with their mother.

"I'm going to see what's going on." Miranda stood and walked across the room toward her husband. After a brief conversation, the Langtry men and Kay left the room.

Miranda returned and sat down on the couch again. "Jesse says it's just a work thing. Nothing to worry about."

Nola had been in the business of reading people for years. You learned how to defend yourself in the Army and always watch your enemy. Once she was stateside again, enrolled in college and majoring in telecommunications with a minor in journalism, she had honed that skill. She could usually tell by the slightest gesture or body language when somebody wasn't telling the truth. The fact that Jesse hadn't looked Miranda in the eyes during their conversation told her this was much more than just business.

After an hour of waiting for Chase to return and three more cups of coffee, Nola wound her way down the hallway to the bathroom. Pumped full of caffeine, she didn't think she'd ever get to sleep that night. She'd stopped to admire the many black-and-white photographs that lined the wall when she heard Chase's voice coming from a partially opened door further down the hall. She peeked through the crack, unobserved by those inside.

"What's he asking for, then?"

"He wants the mineral rights he claims Joe stole from him in addition to a public apology from all of you," Jon said. "I wouldn't be surprised if he adds a dollar figure come tomorrow morning."

"And if we don't comply?" Cole asked.

"Then he goes public," Jon replied.

"Daddy didn't steal anything." Shane slammed his fist down on the mahogany desk. "I've never even heard of this guy before."

"Scott David is a well-known cattle baron just north of Dallas." Jon raked his fingers through his hair. "I don't like this any more than you do, and whether you give him what he wants or not, I don't trust that he's going to stay quiet."

Nola knew she shouldn't eavesdrop, but the mention of Scott David's name glued her to the floor. Now his very public attacks began to make sense.

"Excuse me." Nola pushed the door open further. "I don't mean to interrupt, but I couldn't help but overhear the conversation on my way to the bath-room."

"Aren't you…you're that reporter from Channel 9. What the heck are you doing here?" Jon may have directed the question at Nola, but his eyes were on Shane, looking for confirmation. Shane nodded and everyone looked at her suspiciously.

"I— Yes—I am, but—"

"She's also my girlfriend." Chase narrowed his eyes at Jon before ushering Nola out of the room. He pulled the door behind him, making sure it closed tightly. "I'm sorry to have abandoned you out there. This is just some crazy business stuff we need to deal with and I'm probably going to be in there for a while. I think we should just call it a night."

"I could look into Scott David for you," Nola offered. "Investigating is part of my job."

"Yeah, about that." Chase glanced back at the closed door. "Thank you, but this is just a misun-derstanding. Can I trust you not to repeat what you heard?"

Nola opened her mouth, then quickly closed it, only nodding her response. The feeling of acceptance she'd had earlier was gone. Chase may have referred to her as his girlfriend, but the actions of everyone in that room spoke louder than his words. They thought of her as the ruthless reporter looking for a juicy lead. And if it was true that Joe had stolen someone's land, it certainly would be just the type of story that would propel her toward the coveted co-anchor position.

"Please thank your mom for having me." Nola gave

Chase a quick peck goodbye, already sensing the distance between them. That was okay. Based on the little she'd overheard, Nola didn't think they knew of Scott David's online ramblings. She was wide-awake and itching to get home to uncover more information about him and the story behind the accusations.

Chapter Seven

It was the last day of class for Chase's resident students. He knew he should focus on their performance in the indoor arena, but he hated the way he'd left things with Nola the night before and couldn't get it out of his head. He had all but accused her of being underhanded. Why hadn't he acknowledged her willingness to help his family?

Earlier that morning he'd ordered three dozen pink and red roses, intending to have them delivered to her office. He decided, though, that nothing screamed "weak apology" like the faceless delivery of flowers, and he'd arranged to pick them up instead. After a little wrangling at the studio, he'd managed to track down George's phone number and confirm that Nola was free that night.

Jon's news had put a damper on an otherwise great birthday. Scott David had made it clear through their attorneys that he was out for blood. Even though everyone had dismissed the idea that Joe Langtry would outright steal, the way Chase's mother had retreated into herself after Jon left had caused Chase to wonder if she knew more than she was letting on. He'd planned to discuss it with her over breakfast, but she had already left the house by the time he'd made it downstairs.

Chase regarded Shane on the other side of the arena, cheering on their best student as he rode a full eight seconds atop one of their toughest bucking broncs. The tension between the two brothers had grown over the past twenty-four hours, and Chase attributed it to Jon's remark about Nola.

Shane wasn't the most trusting of people, not that Chase could blame him. None of them really knew Nola outside of her job. The personal side of her was still new to the Langtrys, and up until last night, they'd all enjoyed having her around as much as he did.

By midafternoon, Chase had said goodbye to the last of the students. The Ramblewood tree lighting would begin in a few hours, and he intended to have Nola there by his side. George had promised to text him when they were on their way back to the studio. Seeing his mother's car parked alongside the house, Chase decided it was best he reconfirmed whether Nola would still be welcome.

Downstairs in the family wine cellar, Kay removed bottles of Christmas muscadine wine from their racks and placed them in multisectioned canvas totes.

"Where have you been all day?" Chase asked.

"At the winery checking our holiday inventory. I've decided to serve our wine at the Mistletoe Rodeo dinner and I threw together some gift baskets to raffle off in the tricky tray." Kay pointed to a full tote. "Would you take that upstairs for me, then come back and get this one? I want to get things ready for tonight."

"Speaking of tonight, is Nola still invited?"

"Why wouldn't she be?" Kay asked, perplexed.

"Well, the way Jon accused her of listening at the door for a news story, I wasn't sure."

Kay shook her head. "Jon did no such thing. I think you're reading too much into it. Besides, there's no story to report. This is all a misunderstanding. I'm sure Jon and the rest of our attorneys will sort it out. That's what we pay them for."

The harshness in his mother's tone unsettled Chase. He didn't think he'd ever heard her use the phrase, "That's what we pay them for" before. It was very unlike her to throw their power around.

"Mom, is there something you're not telling us?"

Kay stopped and stared at him. "What I'm telling you is to forget this nonsense and help me carry these upstairs. Call your brothers and tell them to get their patooties over here because I want all the Christmas decorations out of the attic before we leave for the tree lighting. I lost track of time today and I'm behind schedule. Now chop-chop." She clapped her hands for emphasis.

After numerous dusty trips to the attic, Chase needed another shower before catching up with Nola, and now he was running low on time. He'd just finished dressing when he received George's text. After stopping at the florist along the way, he arrived at the television station with only half an hour to convince Nola to accompany him to the tree lighting—preferably alone. He wanted to spend the evening with her, not with her and George.

Her office door was open and he knocked lightly, hiding his face behind the roses. Not hearing the laughter he had hoped for, he slowly lowered the flowers. Nola sat at her desk, her back rigid, face frozen. By no means did she appear amused or in a forgiving mood. In fact, he wasn't quite sure what her mood was. She looked like a statue.

"I'll begin with 'I'm sorry,' but I know that probably doesn't mean much." Chase took a step forward and set the roses on the corner of her desk.

"It helps." Nola looked at the arrangement and inhaled the scent without moving from her seated position. "They're beautiful. Thank you."

"I didn't mean to make you feel uncomfortable last night." Chase sat in the chair across from her. "The news of this Scott David person just really took us by surprise."

"What would you say if I told you I wasn't surprised?" Nola tapped her pen against a file folder in front of her.

"You know Scott David?" Chase knew it was part of Nola's job to be aware of what was going on out there, but he would have thought a cattle baron north of Dallas was out of her news coverage area.

"I know of him." Nola opened her folder, turned it toward him and slid it across the desk. "This is a photo of Scott and his trophy wife, Juanita." Nola flipped the page. "This is his online persona and the avatar he uses when commenting about you and your family."

Chase studied the pictures, both meaning nothing to him. "What comments has he made? And how do you know about him?"

"After your National Finals interview at the ranch, I went online to check the social media sites to see how our segment went over with your fans. That was the first time I saw his comments. Every site I went to, his name was there. And he's made further comments in more places every day since. They're all there. I printed them out."

"This is what you were trying to tell us when you came into the room last night, wasn't it?"

"It was, and I was so annoyed afterward I wasn't even going to give you this much, to tell you the truth." Nola gestured to the flowers again. "Let's just say I had a change of heart."

Chase stood and awkwardly attempted to squeeze between her desk and filing cabinet. "Do you think there might be room for one more change of heart?"

Nola stifled a giggle at his distress. "That all depends on what we're talking about."

"Come to the tree lighting with me and my family. I know you're on standby, and if you have to leave, that's fine. But we would really love to have you come back to our house afterward for food and the tree trimming and caroling and—" Chase crouched before her as best he could with what little room he had and took her hands in his. "Nola, it would mean the world to me to spend this time with you. Christmas is a big deal for my family and I'd love to have you there with us tonight. I think you deserve to celebrate the holiday."

Nola's eyes began to glisten. "I don't know what to say, except…yes. I'd love to."

"Since we've practically spent the past week together, and I think we both enjoy each other's company, I have something else to ask you." Chase squeezed her hands a little tighter, hoping he wouldn't scare her away. "I don't know how you're feeling or where you'd like to see this go, but I'd like to give it a genuine chance. I screwed up last night and that was hard to live with today. So how would you feel about spending the holidays with me and my crazy family? I'd love to show you a real Christmas."

Nola didn't answer in words. Instead, she snaked her arms around his neck and kissed him. Drawing her closer, Chase pulled her to her feet.

"Is that a yes?" The warmth of her body against his sparked other ideas. He'd much rather skip the tree lighting so they could be alone.

"Yes." Nola kissed him again.

Reluctantly he set her away from him. "In that case, we don't have much time."

"Then, let's go." Nola grabbed her red wool coat and her handbag and stood waiting for Chase to lead the way.

"Oh, hell." Chase attempted to squeeze past her desk and filing cabinet again. "You really need a larger office."

"I'm lucky I have this one," Nola said as they entered the hallway.

"And I'm lucky I have you."

Nola shook her head at him. "I never took you for the hopeless-romantic type." Nola pushed open the double doors to the parking lot and began walking to her car. "I'll follow you if I'm going to the ranch afterward. That way we won't have to backtrack here later."

"Okay." Chase hated how the temporary separation cooled their moment. He had looked forward to driving to the tree lighting with Nola beside him in his truck. There was something comforting about the idea. It almost had a sense of permanence to it, and for the first time, Chase wondered if he had found the woman for him.

RAMBLEWOOD WAS PACKED with cars, forcing Nola and Chase to park at Slater's Mill and walk toward the center of town.

"I don't think we'll make it in time." Chase took her hand in his and led her toward the sidewalk. "Want to make a run for it?"

Although Nola had worn pants to work, she was in heels. "I don't think that's going to happen in these shoes. Give me a second to grab my sneakers out of my car."

Chase checked his watch. "There's no time." He turned around, squatted and looked over his shoulder. "Hop on."

Nola laughed at him and continued to her vehicle, unlocking it quickly. "You're insane, you know that? The last thing your shoulder needs is me holding onto it for dear life as you run us down the street." She slipped on a pair of black running shoes, tossed her heels onto the backseat and shut the door. "Let's do this."

Hand in hand, they ran toward Main Street, laughing hysterically along the way. She was impressed that Chase could keep up with her—not many people could. Running was a holdover from her military days and it helped keep her grounded.

"Chase! Nola!" Tess called out through the sea of people. "We were beginning to wonder if you'd make it."

"So were we," Nola said as Tess pulled her into a warm embrace. One day she'd get used to this hugging thing, but it was still new to her. She waved to Chase's brother over Tess's shoulder. "Hi, Cole."

"Good to see you." The man gave her a quick hug. "They're running a little late, so you haven't missed anything."

Relieved that there didn't appear to be any lingering suspicion from last night, Nola began to relax. An enormous white spruce stood in the middle of Ramblewood Park. Nola hadn't imagined the place would be this full. She'd heard of small-town tree-lighting ceremonies before, even seen them in holiday movies, but none of them compared to the sheer magnitude of people who'd come out for this one.

A man stood on the back of a decorated flatbed trailer and tapped the microphone. "Welcome, Ramblewood!" The crowd erupted in applause. "Thank you all for coming out this gorgeous evening. If you wander near the fountain, please help yourself to a free hot chocolate, generously donated by The Dog House. I apologize for the delay, but we had to wait for a few members of our opening act to arrive. Please join me in welcoming the first and second grade classes of Ramblewood Elementary as they lead us into our Christmas celebration."

The crowd applauded again as a large group of children climbed the staircase onto the trailer and faced the crowd. Chase stood behind Nola, wrapping his arms around her like a warm blanket, erasing any doubts she had about him earlier. His nearness heightened her senses, making it easy to get lost in this moment.

"We love you, Ever!" Tess waved to her daughter onstage while Cole recorded them on his phone. Nola had been one of the child's biggest fans since the day they'd met. Ever's cerebral palsy had made walking difficult back then, but her continued hippotherapy and leg braces allowed her to easily walk onstage with the rest of her class tonight.

"They're adorable." Nola clapped and waved along with the crowd as the children sang "Jingle Bells" and "Here Comes Santa Claus."

"I never in a million years would have thought that coming home for Jesse's wedding would take my life in this direction." A tear spilled onto Tess's cheek, her face shining with pure pride for her daughter as she spoke to Nola. "Cole and I dated in high school, but we went our separate ways. When I saw him again, I knew this was where I belonged. Ramblewood was home."

Cole kissed his wife on the cheek. "I'm going to go get Ever. Be right back."

Nola glanced around the large crowd, wanting for once to capture a moment in her mind instead of on camera. The chill of the night air didn't stand a chance of penetrating the warmth that radiated off the people there. She may have avoided the event in the past, but she silently vowed never to miss another one in the future.

After Cole and Ever joined them and a few more performances by local children, everyone began to light the single white candle they had received when they entered the park.

The emcee once again took the stage. "If you would all be so kind, please join me in singing "Silent Night" as we remember those who are no longer with us."

It was a touching gesture, and Nola was aware of a few people wiping away tears. She looked down at Ever standing between Tess and Cole, and then squeezed her eyes tight, willing herself not to cry.

"Are you okay?" Chase whispered against her cheek from behind.

"I will be if you continue to hold me." Chase tightened his arms around Nola and sang into her hair. When the song ended, they blew out their candles as the mass collectively observed a moment of silence.

Kay and the rest of the Langtry clan made their way toward them as they waited for the lighting of the tree. Afraid she might cry if she spoke, Nola managed to hug everyone without uttering a word.

"Ramblewood." The host began to rile the crowd once again. "Please join me in wishing your friends and neighbors a merry Christmas!"

The Christmas tree instantly began to sparkle with thousands of colored lights reflecting off red velvet bows. It might be smaller, but to Nola, this tree beat the one she'd seen online at Rockefeller Center. A seemingly endless stream of strangers hugged and wished her a merry Christmas to the point where Nola thought her heart might burst with happiness.

Chase turned her around in his arms and kissed her. His tongue parted her lips and in the fervor of the moment, Nola forgot where they were. She wasn't big on public displays of affection, but with Chase, all her previous rules seem to fly right out the window. She was breathless when their kiss broke, and when she looked into his eyes Nola felt her heart lurch madly. She didn't know if it was because their relationship was moving on to the next step or if it was the magic of the Christmas spirit surrounding her. At this point, she didn't care. All she knew was that she didn't want it to end.

NOLA DROVE BEHIND Chase on their way to the ranch. He'd never been one to speed, but tonight he couldn't get home quickly enough. He wanted to park his truck, pull Nola from her car and disappear, spending the rest of the night making love to her. His family might kill him, but it would be worth it. He needed to feel Nola in his arms, with nothing between them. He craved that closeness more than he had ever wanted anything in his life.

He pulled up next to the house and Nola parked beside him. "Were we in the Indy 500?" Nola asked as she stepped from the car.

Chase didn't answer her. Instead, he grabbed her hand before she had a chance to retrieve her coat from the car and led her to the rodeo school, knowing no one would be there at this hour.

"What are we doing here?" Nola asked as Chase unlocked the door and held it open for her.

He locked up behind him and tucked Nola against him. "Nothing you don't want to do. I just needed time alone with you. Whenever we're together, there's somebody else around and I wanted a moment for us."

His heart hammered against his rib cage. A hot ache grew in his chest. Dipping his head, his lips brushed hers softly. There was no rush. Chase wanted to take his time and enjoy the feel and the taste of her.

He took her hands in his, encouraging her to explore his body. Following his lead, Nola brushed her fingers against the bare skin under the waistband of his jeans. A shiver of anticipation rocketed through him. Fumbling with the buttons on her shirt in the dark, he opted to lift it over her head. The lace of her bra grazed the pads of his thumbs as they encircled her nipples.

"Tell me to stop and I will," Chase whispered.

"Don't." Nola's voice was thick with desire. "Whatever you do, please, don't stop. I need you."

So much for taking his time.

Those were all the words Chase needed to hear. He unfastened her bra and let it slide slowly from her arms. He was barely able to make out her body, but the moon shining through the building's skylights revealed all he needed to see.

They both took off their shoes, then Nola unhooked his belt buckle with deftness, unbuttoned his jeans and pushed them down past his thighs. He stepped out of his pants and reached for hers, easing them down, trailing kisses between her breasts. Nola lifted his chin before he could kiss her any lower.

"I want to feel you." Her whisper echoed in the darkness of the building's stone entryway. Nola slipped her hand beneath his boxer briefs and wrapped her hand around his arousal. "Good God, you feel amazing."

Chase's mouth hungrily claimed hers as he removed her panties. Shrugging out of his boxer briefs, he growled against her mouth, crushing her against him. He widened his stance to meet her height; his hardness flattened against her sweet spot. Aching to lose himself inside her, Chase shifted Nola until her back was against the door.

Grabbing her thighs, he lifted her, ignoring the pain in his shoulder. Her legs wrapped around his waist, imprisoning his body with hers, replacing any discomfort he felt with desire.

"Please, Chase," Nola groaned. "Now."

And in that moment, as the stars shone through the skylights above them, Chase found heaven.

BREATHLESS AND GIGGLING, Nola fumbled for her clothes in the dark. "Your mother is going to kill us."

"Yeah, but it was so worth it." Chase tugged her back into his arms, his hands immediately seeking her breasts. "Think we could squeeze in another round?"

"No, I do not." Nola wriggled away. "I don't think my shirt survived our little…episode." Even in the moonlight, she could see how dirty her once-white blouse had become. "Do you think you'd be able to sneak out to my car and grab the bag I keep in the backseat? There's a pair of black leggings and a denim shirt in it. At least I could change into something a little cleaner. I don't think anyone will notice—I had my coat on at the tree lighting."

"I'll try, but I can't guarantee I won't get caught. There are eyes everywhere on this ranch, especially my sisters-in-law's." Nola heard Chase pull on his jeans. "I'll lock the door, but I suggest you cover up while I'm gone, just in case."

He closed the door behind him and the deadbolt clicked into place. Standing in the center of the entry-way alone, Nola couldn't believe what had just happened. She'd just unabashedly had sex with Chase. Incredible sex. The best of her life.

She had no idea how they were going to explain their absence. Surely, someone would have seen their cars by now. The last thing she wanted to do was embarrass him. No one wanted their family to know they'd just sneaked away to get it on with their girl-friend. But every excuse she thought of sounded like an outright lie, and she hated the thought of lying to the Langtrys.

The sound of the door opening so soon after Chase had left startled her. Flattening herself against the cold stone wall, Nola gripped her blouse tightly to her chest.

"Where are you?" Chase asked from the doorway.

Nola exhaled the breath she'd been holding. "You scared me half to death. How did you get back here so fast?"

"I ran." Chase closed the door behind him and handed her the bag. "You didn't think I was going to take my time with you standing in here naked, did you?"

"Did anyone see you?" Nola reached inside for her shirt and leggings.

"Not that I noticed." Chase attempted to pull her into his arms again. "There's no reason to be nervous. Even if they did, it doesn't matter."

Nola playfully slapped his hands away. "It does matter. I don't want your family to think I'm a floozy."

"No one is going to think you're a floozy." Chase stilled her hands and gathered her against his body. "Why would you even think that?"

"Your mom's been so generous with me. I don't want her to think I'm taking advantage of you."

"And here I was afraid you'd think I had taken advantage of you." His calloused hands cupped her face and held it gently. "Nola, my family will never judge you. I promise."

"I trust you." At least she thought she did. She

wanted to. Nola knew one day she would need to tell Chase about her past, but now wasn't the right moment. There was time, and if Chase was right in thinking no one would judge her, why should her past matter anyway? Love meant acceptance, and although Nola wasn't sure if they'd ever reach that stage, tonight gave her reason to believe they were heading in the right direction.

"Please don't ever doubt me," Chase whispered against her mouth before their lips met. The comforting strength of his arms melted away her fears of rejection. "I hate letting you go, but we should head up to the main house before they send out a search party."

"We don't want that." Nola finished dressing, missing his touch as she did.

She dropped her bag off in the car on the way to the house, still uncertain how to explain where they'd been. Nola wasn't even sure how long they'd been gone.

"It's about time you two showed up." Lexi looked them both up and down as they walked into the kitchen. "Oh. My. God. You two got into the spirit of things, didn't you?" She made a tsk sound with her tongue. "Good for you. Come join the rest of the party. I'm sure you must be hungry."

What the heck?

"How did she know?" Nola couldn't believe her ears. "Did we just get congratulated for having sex?"

"Yes, we did. And it's called afterglow." Chase rested his hand on the small of her back, guiding her through the kitchen to the great room. "I told you there was nothing to worry about."

"Nola, Chase, grab a sandwich and something to drink from the buffet and help us decorate the tree." If Kay suspected anything, the older woman didn't let on.

There were a few knowing winks and nods from the Langtry siblings and their wives, but it was all in good fun. Nola excused herself to the bathroom to make sure she was presentable after getting dressed in the dark. When she came out, Chase handed her an empty plate. She'd been so busy today she'd forgotten to eat, and after what they'd just been up to, she had definitely worked up an appetite.

"I'm ravenous," Nola said.

"That you are," Chase whispered against her ear before kissing her cheek.

"You're bad," Nola teased. "And I like it."

They filled their plates and joined the rest of the family around the tree. Within minutes, Nola's uncertainties waned and she began to enjoy herself. She'd always wondered what Christmas felt like when you didn't have a family full of issues. She could get used to this. It was noisy and filled with laughter, the sounds of what a home should be…especially a home at Christmas. Nola wanted this life for herself and she wanted it with Chase.

Chapter Eight

"He's after the ranch, isn't he?" Cole perched on the edge of his chair in attorney Jon Reese's office, flanked by Chase, Shane and their mother. "Why else would he ask for a hundred million dollars?"

"No judge in this state will award him that. He's on a fishing expedition to see if you'll bite." Jon leaned forward on his desk and tapped his fingertips together. "I'm waiting for Kenny Gilbert to join us. He personally handled the financial aspects of every one of Joe's land acquisitions."

"A judge *could* award him something and eventually bankrupt us." Shane paced the law office like a caged lion.

"Only if he could prove that Joe knowingly took advantage of other people," Jon said. "He'd need a court order to have access to Bridle Dance's financial records or to Joe's personal files, and that would never happen. Only the state could prosecute that type of case, and Scott David would need a mountain of evidence against Joe even to get his foot in the door. There are too many factors involved for it ever to materialize."

"If he can't get any money out of us and doesn't have any evidence, then what's the point?" Chase couldn't understand how a man could appear out of nowhere and make false claims against his father without any proof to back them up.

"I never said he couldn't get any money from you. Since Joe is no longer alive, and none of you were involved in the running of the ranch back in 2008, the only thing I can foresee him getting are the mineral rights. Other than that, I believe Scott David is making these threats in the hopes that you'll make him an offer to shut him up."

"Shut up about what?" Kay rose from her chair in front of Jon's desk. "Joe acquired those mineral rights legally. I refuse to stand by and watch some jackass come into my town and tarnish my husband's good name. Over my dead body."

"Mom." Chase reached for Kay only to be swatted away. "You need to calm down."

"Don't you tell me to calm down." Kay's face reddened, worrying Chase that her blood pressure was spiking out of control.

Afraid to anger her further, he leaned back in his chair and tried to wrap his head around the situation. "If Scott David's grandfather still owns the surface rights to the land, why does it matter if we own the mineral rights?"

"Because the mineral estate becomes the dominant estate," Jon said. "That means the surface estate exists for the benefit of the mineral owner—in this case, Bridle Dance—and grants them certain entitlements."

"In layman's terms, if Scott wants to run cattle on that land and we want to mine it, we could essentially halt his operation," Cole explained.

"I don't think you'd be doing any mining," Jon said. "Those fifty thousand acres are on the outskirts of the Eagle Ford Shale. If you were doing anything, you'd be fracking for natural gas or oil."

"That would explain why Dad bought land that wasn't anywhere near Bridle Dance." Chase began to see the purchase through his father's eyes. Those acres might have billions of dollars' worth of oil under them. "Maybe he knew what was beneath it."

"I've gone ahead and ordered a geological study." Jon slid a piece of paper across the desk. "This is the name of the company I'm using and their phone number if you want to contact them. Once we receive their report, we'll know more. I'm betting Scott already performed a study on his own and he knows what's down there. He may want what's underneath for himself, or he may want to prevent environmental damage. That may be why he's fighting so hard for it.

"If you frack, or fracture, the land adjacent to where he's running cattle, the enormous amounts of water, sand and chemicals that are used to stimulate the gas production in the well can contaminate the groundwater. That would be detrimental to his cattle operation, and it could also affect the value of his land and the people's health on neighboring ranches."

"What if we give him back the mineral rights

now?" Shane asked. "Will that end this before it gets out of hand?"

"Don't you dare give him anything," Kay ordered. "If there is oil or gas on that land, you can't just hand it over because someone says, 'Boo.'"

Chase hadn't seen his mother this angry in years, and the feeling he had that she knew more than she was saying increased further.

"Mom, you're here because this involves Dad's reputation," Cole stated firmly. "But please keep in mind that it's not your decision to make. It's ours. The four of us own Bridle Dance. For the life of me, I still can't understand why you allowed Daddy to set it up that way, but you did. I'm not saying we won't take your feelings into consideration, but if there's an easy way to end this, we need to do it."

Kay shook her head at Cole, but before she could respond there was a knock at Jon's office door. Kenny Gilbert entered, armed with a stack of file folders.

"I'm sorry I'm late, but I needed to double-check a few things." Kenny placed the stack on Jon's desk and flipped open the first folder. "When I heard the name Scott David, I knew it sounded familiar. Joe and Scott had a history dating back twenty years. They repeatedly went up against each other on land acquisitions, and since Bridle Dance had more buying power, Joe outbid him nearly every time. Especially in the beginning when Scott didn't have much to work with."

"So this is a grudge match?" Shane asked while looking over the papers.

"One potentially worth billions." Kenny handed out copies of documents to everyone. "As Bridle Dance acquired better land for their horses, Scott David wanted it for his cattle operation. He was ruthless and determined to win at any cost, and he went after some land adjacent to yours. I'm talking twenty years ago. When Joe outbid him, Scott went to the landowner and lied about Joe's intentions, claiming Joe had planned to get it rezoned for a shopping center."

Chase flipped through the pages, trying to make sense of it all. "He just believed what Scott said without checking with my father?"

"Yes, and he sold the land to Scott at a much lower price. It became an all-out war, and then Joe targeted Nate David, Scott's grandfather. He went after the land Scott would inherit, knowing it would hurt him. Nate refused for years, but when the rumor of the Eagle Ford Shale's existence was just beginning to spread, Joe convinced Nate to sell him the mineral rights. It was a sly investment on your father's part, but it wasn't illegal."

"I'm a little lost. What does the Eagle Ford Shale have to do with anything?" Kay asked.

"The shale is one of the most actively drilled areas for oil and natural gas in the country," Kenny answered. "Its discovery seven years ago was a game changer for the industry."

"Why did Nate finally decide to sell the rights?" Chase knew his father could hold a grudge—but for twenty years? It seemed excessive, even for Joe.

"Because Joe had always targeted the entire estate up until that point. With the mineral rights severed from the estate, Nate would still have the land to hand down to Scott. The sale of the mineral rights gave Nate the cash he needed to finance his retirement and cover future assisted-living-facility expenses. According to Scott, his grandfather had already been diagnosed with Alzheimer's when he signed over those rights."

"The fact that Nate knew he needed to prepare for the future tells me he was still of sound mind," Jon said. "There may or may not have been anything wrong with him back in 2008 when this transpired. Scott's banking on us not knowing the answer to that question."

"Where is Nate now?" Kay asked, calmer than before.

"In a nursing home." Jon flipped through the notes on his legal pad. "He only went in there last year. Up until that point, he'd been living in his own house. That's a big chunk of time for somebody who allegedly couldn't make decisions on his own. The man even did his own banking and paid his own bills."

"How do you know that?" Chase asked.

"I had Clay Tanner run a preliminary background check on Nate and Scott David," Jon replied. "I want you all to go home, put this out of your heads for the rest of the weekend and let me see what else I can dig up. I need to review all of these files with Kenny, and as soon as I know more, I'll give you a call. I don't think Scott's going to do anything immediately—he's waiting for you to make a deal for his silence, and he knows he has to be careful. We could go after him for slander if he doesn't have anything to substantiate his claims."

The Langtrys rode back to the ranch together in silence. The fact that his father had known Scott David and had battled him for two decades concerned Chase. He didn't want to believe that his father had taken advantage of Nate David, and it bugged him that he was giving any weight to Scott's claims. If this man could create doubt in his own family, how would the rest of Ramblewood react? The memory of a man so revered could be destroyed in a heartbeat.

When they arrived at the ranch, Kay climbed out of the SUV and headed into the house. Bridle Dance was supposed to lead the Winter Festival parade that afternoon with his mother at the reins of the buckboard. Now Chase wondered if she even wanted to go.

"You boys get things together and give me a few minutes." His mother looked around the ranch, worry from the morning's events etched into her forehead. "I'll be out to help shortly."

"Mom, we have everything." Cole approached her, pulling her into an embrace. "I'm sorry for the way I spoke earlier. I know this situation upsets you. It upsets all of us. We'll do everything in our power to protect Dad's name."

Wordlessly Kay touched Cole's cheek, and a single tear trailed down hers as she turned and walked into the house. She didn't deserve this kind of anguish. It was bad enough she'd lost her husband so young, but whatever issue Scott David had with the family, he could have had some respect for the fact that the man had been someone's husband and father.

"I'm going to bring the horse trailers around. I'll meet you two out there." Cole walked away, leaving Chase alone with Shane.

Shane regarded Chase for a moment, then shook his head. "Come on. Let's get these horses ready."

"Can we talk for a minute?" Chase ventured.

"What's on your mind?" Shane continued walking toward the stables.

"I'm not really sure how to say this." Chase hesitated.

"Just say it." Shane stopped and looked him directly in the eyes. "The last I checked I don't bite, although you wouldn't know it the way you've been acting the last little while."

"I'm done with the rodeo," Chase blurted out. "My last ride took a lot out of me and I'm afraid of permanently damaging my shoulder."

Shane crossed his arms. "I wondered when you were going to tell me."

"You knew?" Chase exhaled slowly, trying to remain calm. "Who told you?"

"Mom," Shane said matter-of-factly. "Not that she meant to, so don't get mad at her. She was concerned about the two of us and it just slipped out."

Chase hadn't considered how much pressure he'd put on his mother when he had confided in her. "I'm not going to make a public announcement until after the first of the year. Cole wanted me to be sure."

"So Cole knew, but your business partner at the rodeo school didn't?" Hurt was evident in Shane's face. "Do you know how that makes me feel?"

"I know this will affect the school—"

"You're damn right it will." Shane balled his fists. "We need to have an instructor who's not only active in the rodeo but who's also a top-ranking competitor. Without that draw, we're just like any other school."

Chase quickly realized that talking to Shane today of all days had been a mistake. "I've made up my mind—don't try to change it. I don't want to do it anymore, and even if I did, it's not worth the risk."

Chase continued walking toward the stables. They needed to prep and load eighteen horses for transport to the festival. The brothers always personally handled the job, never leaving the grooms accountable for the horses' safety.

"I never realized how little you thought of me," Shane called after him.

Chase spun around. "This has nothing to do with you—it's about me. It's about what I want, my health and my future."

"You're not getting it, Chase!" Shane shouted, his voice reverberating off the side of the building. "I don't care about the rodeo. I care that you didn't feel comfortable enough to come to me with your decision. I would never try to change your mind. I'm glad Mom told me, because if she hadn't, and you'd waited until the new year, any chance we had of snagging one of the top-ten riders at Nationals would've been gone. And you're not going to want to hear this, but I've already set up interviews."

"You did what?" Shane had no right to tell anyone Chase was leaving the circuit. It was Chase's decision and his announcement. "How dare you?"

"How dare I?" Shane took a step closer. "How dare you put this business at risk? How dare you put the money our father left us in jeopardy because of your selfishness? And before you get your jockey shorts in a wad, no one knows you're retiring. They only know we're looking to bring in an additional instructor, possibly two."

"Any hiring decisions have to be mutual," Chase demanded.

"I wouldn't have it any other way." Shane stared at him. "You, on the other hand, want to keep things from me. Yet I'm the bad guy. I'm not the same person I was years ago. Other people have put it in the past—you haven't yet. I don't get that. Why did you go into business with me if you didn't trust me?"

"I do trust you." *To a point.* Chase had seen how destroyed his mother had been back when Shane had attempted to prevent the building of Dance of Hope. The memory was hard to erase. "You're right. I'm not being fair. Today in Jon's office reminded me of when we were there three years ago fighting over this business."

"We were fighting *against* one another then." Shane gripped Chase's shoulders. "We're supposed to be on the same side. We *need* to be for Mom's sake and for our father's legacy. I know this was a big deci-

sion for you and I'm fine with it. I love you and I want
you to do what's best for you. Work with me—don't
keep things from me. Dammit, Chase, we're family."

Chase nodded, a lump forming in his throat. They
slapped each other on the back and continued into
the stables.

NOLA WAS DUE to arrive shortly. He'd asked her to stay
over after the tree trimming party, but she hadn't felt
comfortable spending the night with Kay down the
hall. He respected her decision, but it didn't make
missing her any easier. The last thing he wanted was
for her to witness more family tension. Although
maybe it would lessen her idyllic view of life at Bridle Dance.

A part of him couldn't help but wonder if Nola was
attracted solely to him, or to some fantasy version of
his lifestyle. Chase knew she wasn't interested in him
for his money. That wasn't even a second thought. But
the fairy-tale aspect worried him.

She'd never said the words aloud. It was the look
on her face when she was with them. Like a kid seeing the Magic Kingdom at Disney World for the
first time. Maybe it was a result of having moved
around so much as a child. There was something to
be said for growing up in the same town with the
same friends your entire life. It brought a sense of
comfort he couldn't imagine living without. But nobody was perfect, and Chase didn't want to let Nola
down. She'd come to mean more to him than he'd
ever thought possible.

A week ago, he had felt horrible at the thought of turning thirty with no prospect of a wife and family. Now he was beginning to see a future with Nola. Chase laughed to himself. Maybe fairy tales did come true.

NOLA COULDN'T BELIEVE she was riding on the back of a buckboard with the rest of the Langtry women and their children. She was dressed in a sparkly blue satin cape and white faux fur Russian hat. Kay, dressed as Mrs. Claus, led a team of horses with silver head-dresses through the center of town. Chase, wearing white sheepskin chaps and a blue Western vest matching her cape, rode horses alongside the wagon with his brothers as they waved to the crowd during the Winter Festival parade. Nola had been in plenty of parades before, but she'd always been in uniform. Today she actually felt pretty and feminine.

At the end of the route, Chase dismounted, handed the reins to one of the grooms and lifted Nola off the buckboard. Cupping her face between his hands, he kissed her softly. "I need to take care of the horses. Will you wait for me?"

"You two go and enjoy yourselves," Shane said. "Lexi and I have this covered. Show Nola what Christmas in Ramblewood is all about."

"Thank you." After the argument Chase had told her he'd had with Shane, Nola was surprised he was willing to help them out this afternoon. Chase hadn't offered up the details, but he had said he hadn't given Shane enough credit.

"That was sweet of him." Nola's smile broadened at the thought of more time with Chase.

"Are you still free for the rest of the afternoon, or has work called?" Chase's breath grazed her lips as he kissed her again.

"Don't jinx it," Nola warned. "I'm looking forward to today."

Nola began to remove her cape and hat when Chase stopped her. "Oh, no, you don't. They stay on. You are a part of the festival with the rest of us. Wear it proudly."

Nola glanced around the street, feeling awkward until she caught sight of others still in costume. "When in Rome…"

Chase slipped his hand in hers, their fingers laced together as they strolled through the streets. Large crystallized snowflakes and icicles hung from above, while cloths in pale shades of ice blue and silver draped elegantly over tables, giving Ramblewood an ethereal feel. Everything glittered and sparkled, reminding her of the ice palace in *Dr. Zhivago*.

"This is truly beautiful." Nola spun around, attempting to commit it all to memory. Come Monday morning, once she was back to her daily grind, she'd wonder if today had truly happened or if it had been a dream. "I love how everyone in town comes together for these festivals. I've heard about them, but I never imagined anything to this extent."

"I don't understand why you've never come with your cousin." Chase entwined his fingers with hers again.

"I think because when it was all over with, I'd have to go home on my own. Spending a day surrounded by laughter and happiness, then walking into the dead silence of my condo would only make me feel lonely. The absence of another beating heart can sometimes be a painful reminder of what we don't have. Avoid the situation and avoid the pain."

"What if I said you didn't have to go home alone tonight?" Chase tugged her to him.

Warmth spread through Nola's body, straight to her heart. "Are you volunteering?"

"When it comes to you, I'm always volunteering." Chase dipped his head for a kiss. "I never want you to feel alone."

"There's my maid of honor." Kylie's high-pitched voice startled them both.

"We will definitely pick up where we left off later on," Chase whispered in Nola's ear.

"I love that color on you. If Aaron and I get married in the spring that would be the perfect color for your dress. I can't wait to go shopping. Please tell me you'll come with me—we can make a day of it. There's a huge bridal shop in San Antonio I'd like to visit, but I'll have to book us in. I guess you have to make an appointment to get into all the boutiques, don't you? Why am I asking you? You've never been married before. But you will be. Just not before me."

Nola shook her cousin's shoulder. "Kylie, breathe."

"I used to think she was wound up before, but ever since I proposed it's gotten worse." Aaron shrugged. "What am I going to do? I can't imagine my life without her in it."

"Hanson's Hardware has earplugs." Chase nudged

Aaron. "You can get a ten pack for three dollars. I'll get you some for a wedding gift."

Nola slapped Chase's arm. "That's not nice. Funny, but not nice."

"Keep it up and I'll make you wear a big old Scarlett O'Hara dress to my wedding." Kylie waggled a finger at Nola.

"Scarlett O'Hara, huh?" Nola looked at Chase and they broke into laughter.

"What's so funny?" Kylie asked Aaron, and he shook his head in response.

"We're not laughing at you." Nola attempted to catch her breath. "It's just an inside joke between Chase and me."

It was funny how those words came so naturally to her. *Chase and me.* Nola had always been jealous when she heard other couples talk about their inside jokes because she had never experienced such a thing. She had never experienced any stable relationship— no sooner would she get involved with someone than she'd have to move away again. It had been the story of her life, and as much as she'd tried to convince herself she never wanted to be rooted to one place permanently, now she yearned for it.

She liked the idea of being close with the same friends ten years from now. She liked having family nearby, in a town where everyone knew everybody else. If the Langtrys weren't in her life, she'd probably be at the studio at that very moment, editing a story to death.

"Nola, are you all right?" Kylie asked. "Why don't

you take a walk with me and we'll let the men do their thing."

"Chase." Aaron deepened his voice. "What do you think of this year's tuxedos?"

Chase shot Nola a questioning look, and she let him know she was okay with a wave of her hand as Kylie led her in the other direction.

"What's going on?" Kylie asked. "One minute you looked like you were on top of the world, and the next you came crashing down."

"Something like that," Nola said.

"Are you worried Chase will find out about what happened?"

Nola's eyes flew open. "Y-you know? You can't possibly."

Kylie nodded. "We knew when it happened. Nola, you were in the hospital for a long time. Of course your parents told us. We weren't sure if you were going to make it."

"You never said anything. Not a word. Why?" Nola asked, her mind reeling with bewilderment.

"It was a sensitive subject." Kylie looked around to make sure nobody was listening. "Let's head toward the park where it's a little more private."

Nola hadn't thought her parents had told anyone about the accident—they'd barely spoken to her about it. Talking about it would mean admitting their daughter wasn't perfect.

Nola followed Kylie to the top of the bleachers and sat down.

"How do you really feel about Chase? Put everything and everyone else aside. What are your feelings today about him?"

The joy she'd experienced only moments ago began to erode. "I like the idea of Chase, but I'm not sure I can be the person he wants."

"How do you know that?" Kylie asked. "Have you discussed the accident with him?"

Nola shook her head. It wasn't a subject she could easily slide into casual banter.

"I've known Chase and the Langtrys my entire life. They are nothing if not honest. Not confiding in him would hurt him more than knowing the truth. You two can get past it."

Nola couldn't believe who she was talking to. The airhead cousin she had always loved to pick on had grown into an intelligent woman. "When did you get so smart?"

"When you work the front desk of a salon all day, you have a ton of magazine articles to read. Plus I'm two years older than you are, so I'm always going to know more than you."

Nola knew her cousin was right about sharing her past with Chase. "I just need to summon the courage to actually say the words." If Chase truly cared for her, then he would accept her for who she was, scars and all.

"I don't know how far you two have taken your relationship." Kylie held Nola's hands in hers. "And it's none of my business, but before you get in any deeper, you need to tell Chase you can't have children."

Chapter Nine

Chase had been thrown a bit when Nola decided to go home alone after the winter festival. She'd just finished telling him how much she disliked doing just that.

He sat in the parking lot of Nola's condo building the next morning, looking up at her window. Maybe the holiday overload was too much for her. Which would mean the surprises he had in the back of his truck might not be the best remedy.

He started the engine and shifted into gear. Chances were she wouldn't even be up this early on a Sunday, and she might not thank him for calling her to find out. He could head back to the ranch and call her a few hours from now, but since he was already here…

Chase shut the engine off once again and climbed out of the truck. He'd buzz her unit and feel her out from there. If she was into the whole Christmas thing, then he'd run out to the truck.

A man exiting the building held the door open for Chase. Although he appreciated the gesture, he thought it defeated the purpose of having a secure building. Deciding against calling from downstairs, he made his way to Nola's door.

Chase knocked lightly, figuring if she was asleep in the bedroom then she wouldn't hear him. The chain on the lock clamored against the door a few seconds later.

"Chase, what are you doing here?" Nola stood in the doorway with her hair in a messy ponytail and wearing a T-shirt and yoga pants. She stepped aside as he entered her tiny kitchen area.

"I didn't wake you, did I?" Chase noticed papers scattered across the dining room table. "I sat out in the parking lot debating whether it was too early."

"Ah, so that was your truck I heard out there. Were you planning on leaving without stopping in?" Nola held up a coffee mug, wordlessly asking if he wanted a cup.

"Yes, please. And please tell me you have regular."

"Sorry, only gingerbread and chocolate mint."

Chase watched a slow smile spread across her delicate features. He liked Nola West without a stitch of makeup. "I sincerely hope you're kidding."

"The only coffee here is French roast. That's all I ever buy."

Nola poured him a cup out of a carafe, something he hadn't seen in his mother's house for years. He rather missed those days, especially when they had a crowd of people over. You shouldn't have to wait in line to get a cup of coffee in your own home.

Chase walked toward the dining room table. "I

didn't mean to interrupt your work." Chase noticed the name Scott David written across the top of one of the papers and turned it around. He picked up another sheet with his father's name on it. "Nola, what is this? Why are you researching my family?"

"I don't know if you could really call it research." Nola handed him his cup and moved to the head of the table. "This guy came out of nowhere and began bashing your family publicly a year ago, but it escalated the minute you left the National Finals Rodeo."

"Scott and my father have a history, and it's not a very pretty one."

"So you do know who he is."

"In a manner of speaking." Chase debated how much he should tell Nola. He wanted to trust her, but the sheer amount of information she had amassed on his family unsettled him. "We met with our attorney yesterday morning and discovered a few things. Over a period of twenty years or so, my dad and Scott battled for control of various pieces of land. One of those properties belonged to Scott's grandfather."

"But he didn't steal it." Nola made it more of a statement than a question.

"It's not even about the land. Scott still owns the surface rights. My father purchased the mineral rights."

"That land doesn't even border your property."

Chase shook his head for a moment. "How would you know that? I never told you where the property was."

"It's all a matter of public record." Nola handed

him a sheet of paper. "This is a list of Bridle Dance properties within the state of Texas that don't border the ranch. When I checked the deeds on each one, I saw the previous owners' names. Nate David was the former mineral rights owner on this one." Nola pointed to the middle of the page. "I've been trying to figure out why your father purchased them."

"I didn't even realize we owned this much away from the ranch." Chase placed the page back on the table and sifted through a few others. Here was yet another reason to get more involved in the family business. He should know all of this. The realization that Nola had enough information on his family for a feature story began to sicken him. "Are you doing a story on my father?"

"I considered it."

The paperwork slipped from his hands to the table.

"The thought lasted all of two seconds," Nola continued. "Then I decided against it. I'm hoping I can help you figure this all out."

Chase gathered up a handful of papers and neatly stacked them. "Your investigation into my family makes me a little uncomfortable."

Nola took the documents from him. "I think there's more to Scott David than what's in here. I wanted to give something back to your family by finding out more about him."

Chase dragged his hands down his face. "I asked you the other day to leave this alone. You can't help when you don't have all the details."

"So why don't you fill me in?"

He stared at her. She honestly didn't seem to think she was crossing the line. Chase was starting to understand Jon's concern over Nola being a reporter.

"I get it now." Nola gathered all her notes and thrust them against his chest. "You don't trust me, do you? I can't do this—I can't be in a relationship with someone who has zero faith in me or my ethics."

"You just said you had considered running a story about my father." Chase clutched the papers. "What do you expect me to do with that statement?"

"I expect you to take it for what it was." Nola bent forward, placing both hands on the table in front of her. "I thought about it, and I thought better of it. I didn't do it."

"But you continued to look into it."

"Only to help you," she argued.

Chase set the documents on the counter and took her hands in his. "This is personal, Nola. How would you like it if I dug into your past? Looking over who you are and all the business dealings you'd had over the years. Maybe I'd find a skeleton or two in your closet."

"I don't even know what to say to that." Nola slipped past him and sat on the couch, drawing her knees to her chest.

Chase had obviously hit a nerve, although he wasn't quite sure which one. He followed her into the living room and sat beside her. "What is this really about?"

Nola tightened the grip on her knees, causing her knuckles to turn white. "I've given you reason not to trust me, and while it was never my intention, I understand where you're coming from."

"I quit the rodeo." The enormous weight that lifted from his chest when he said the words surprised even Chase.

"What?" Nola's mouth fell open.

"This is me trusting you." Chase wanted—needed—Nola to feel secure with him and if that meant baring part of his soul in order to prove himself, then he'd do it. "My agent doesn't even know about it yet. Only Cole, Shane and my mother do."

"But why?"

Chase spent the next hour filling Nola in on the full details of his injury and his desire to have a family like his brothers did. He admitted his shame not only for neglecting to carry his weight where Bridle Dance was concerned, but also for his utter failure to become the one thing his father had groomed him to be. A champion.

"I realize I never met the man, but I'd like to believe if your father were alive today, he would understand why you retired." Nola rested her hand on his thigh.

"It's not just my injury. I think I would've done it anyway to help my brother out."

"You can't know that. If your father was still alive, Cole might not have retired yet. Or maybe he would've won the championship already. In fact, you wouldn't even have the business to worry about because your father would still be running it. If the operation of the ranch wasn't in play, do you think you'd still be retiring today?"

Chase hadn't looked at it that way. The reality was that his father *was* gone and the ranch *was* their responsibility. It had just taken him longer than Cole to realize it.

"I probably would. I don't necessarily know if I'd go into business with my father. He was a very… I don't want to say controlling man, but he could be difficult to work for. I can see where we would've butted heads. I don't know. Let's just say I'm retiring because I don't want to do it anymore."

"As long as it's for the right reasons." Nola turned to face him, resting her back against the arm of the couch. "If you truly don't want to compete anymore, that's a great reason to stop. If it's your injury…again, a great reason. But if you're quitting because you feel obligated to Cole, don't. That will only make you resent him in the end and you'll be doing a disservice to him and to yourself."

"I understand what you're saying and I promise to think it over." Chase sighed, not sure he wanted to hear the answer to the question he was about to ask. "Nola, what happened yesterday? We were having a great time and then you shut down on me. I know I've been shoving Christmas down your throat, and I'm sorry if it's been too much for you."

"It hasn't. Honestly, Chase, I've loved every second of it. You have no idea how much spending time with you and your family has meant to me. The way they've welcomed me— Your family's amazing. I'm in awe of how much they've always supported you. I wish I had that, but my family is different and that will never change. I've accepted it. Yesterday I just needed a moment to let it all sink in."

Chase noticed there wasn't a single photo of anyone in her condo. There wasn't even a painting or any wall decorations. The room was bare and cold.

"So you're not against Christmas, then?" Chase asked.

"Not at all. I've just never had much of a reason to celebrate it before."

"Wait right here." Chase stood up and ran to the door. "I'll be back in a minute."

NOLA WATCHED HIM GO, kicking herself for passing up the opportunity to tell him the truth about her past. He'd confided in her, yet she hadn't been able to summon the strength to do the same.

The entry intercom sounded and Nola buzzed Chase back upstairs. Holding the door for him, she couldn't believe her eyes when she saw him carrying a Christmas tree in one arm and a variety of bags in the other.

"Chase, what is all of this?"

"This, my dear, is a Christmas tree. I don't know how you are with plants because I don't see any here, but you need to water it every day or else you'll end up with a pile of needles on your floor within the week. Where would you like me to set it up?"

"I can't believe you did this!" Nola followed Chase to the living room. "In front of the window, I guess."

Chase set his armload on the floor and dug out a tree stand. "Will you help guide me in?"

Nola froze and then stared at Chase, causing them to break into laughter. "At least we know we both have dirty minds."

With the tree firmly in place, they began to sort through the decorations he'd bought.

"Normally you would collect ornaments over the years but considering this is your first tree—well, at least your first tree with me—I figured we needed to start somewhere. Do you like your lights flashing or just a steady on?"

"Flashing lights give me a headache." Nola laughed.

"Steady it is." Together they wrapped the strands of lights around the tree, then added the ornaments until there were no bare limbs left.

Standing back, Nola admired their handiwork. "It's beautiful."

"We're not done yet." Chase removed a silver and gold star from a bag. "It's not an official Christmas tree without a star or an angel on the top. After the other night, I know you're definitely no angel, and the stars reminded me of the ones looking down on us through the skylights while I made love to you."

"You most definitely are a hopeless romantic." Nola took the star from his hands. "Thank you for doing all of this."

"Get moving. You need to put that star on there before we move to stage two."

"Stage two?"

"Nola, the star."

Stretching all the way up onto her toes, Nola slipped the decoration on the very top of the tree. "Is it on straight?"

"Looks it to me. Come back here and see for yourself." Chase held out his arm, inviting Nola to tuck herself against his body. "Do you like it?"

"I love it." Nola wrapped her arms tightly around his waist, pressing her cheek against his shoulder. "I love everything about this moment."

"Then, you're also going to love what comes next." Chase retrieved one of the shopping bags and held it open for Nola to peek inside.

"I've always wanted to make one of these!" She excitedly removed the gingerbread kit from the bag. "There's a lot to this little house. It looks complicated."

"If you can pass basic training, you can build a gingerbread house." Chase took the box and sliced it open with his pocketknife. "Let's clear off the table."

For the next couple of hours, Nola and Chase built one of the most intricate gingerbread houses she'd ever seen. Not that she was an expert, but she thought they'd done a pretty good job. When it was completed Nola went to her bedroom to fetch her camera so she could take a picture. Turning around, she found Chase standing in the doorway.

"I was just curious to see where you slept."

Nola followed his eyes around the room. There wasn't much to look at. She'd learned over the years to travel light, and she didn't own many personal possessions.

"Nice camera. My father loved photography. He took most of the photos displayed in our house."

Nola turned the 35mm camera over in her hands. "It's been all over the world with me. I guess you could say I'm a hobby photographer."

"Yet you don't have a single picture anywhere." Chase tilted his head as if he was trying to figure her out.

"I like to look at them onscreen every now and then, but I don't like a constant visual reminder of what once was."

Chase took a step toward her, removing the camera from her hands and setting it on the dresser. Tilting her chin up to him, he kissed her lips gently. "Who hurt you so badly?"

Nola closed her eyes, willing back the tears that threatened to spill forth at any moment.

"I promise never to hurt you." Chase kissed her cheeks, then her neck, slowly easing the neckline of her T-shirt to the side and trailing more kisses across her collarbone.

Nola ran her hands across the front of his thermal shirt, enjoying the way the muscles flexed beneath her fingertips. He was strong and virile and Nola felt safe in his arms. She loosened his top from his waistband and slid her hands beneath it, enjoying the smooth lines of his skin.

Chase lifted his shirt over his head and tossed it onto the bed. Gripping the sides of her T-shirt, he did the same. Nola immediately dropped her gaze to the floor. Hearing Chase gasp and sensing his hesitation, she couldn't bear to meet his eyes. She knew he could see the scars crisscrossing her chest and abdomen. They would always be there, serving as a constant reminder of what she had done. Without a word, Chase eased her onto the bed and cupped her breasts over her bra. Her flesh ached, begging to be touched.

Chase gently removed the remainder of her clothing and Nola lay on the bed before him more exposed than she'd ever been with anyone. She watched as he removed his own clothes, then stood at the foot of the bed. Starting at her toes, Chase slowly kissed his way toward her mouth, causing a tormented groan to escape her throat. His hard body rose above hers as he slowly inched his way between her thighs.

Lost in the moment, Nola rode the wave of pleasure along with him. When it was over, Chase pulled her into his arms, and she rested her head against his beating heart. The sound was one she could easily get used to.

"Tell me what happened to you," Chase whispered against her hair.

"I was in a car accident and I was thrown through the windshield." Nola felt Chase stiffen.

"That had to have been horrible." His fingers gently combed her hair. "How did it happen?"

"I was eighteen, having a really tough time in another new school and I got involved with the wrong crowd." Chase continued to stroke her hair while he listened. "My parents and I had gotten into an argument that night and I stole a bottle of Dad's vodka."

Chase's hand stilled. "Nola, no."

"I had the radio blaring, one hand on the steering wheel and the other on the bottle. I had probably drunk half of it when I hit another car. They say I was going seventy miles an hour when I was ejected. The woman I hit lost one of her legs. The doctors never thought I'd survive the first week. I was in a medically induced coma while I healed."

"Your parents had to have been frantic." Chase pulled her tighter to him. "Were they angry? Is that why you don't have much of a relationship with them nowadays?"

Nola knew if she didn't tell Chase the truth, the whole truth right now, she might never have the nerve. "When they had me admitted into the hospital they discovered I was three months pregnant. I'd had no idea—I only learned about it after they brought me out of my coma. There was no possible way my baby could have survived the impact I sustained." Nola heard Chase's heartbeat quicken and she began to shiver. "That was also when they told me they'd performed an emergency hysterectomy and I would never be able to have children."

Chase's entire body went rigid. Nola pressed her face to his chest, too afraid to see the disappointment in his expression—the disappointment and the disgust for what she'd done. When the pain of lying next to him, waiting for him to speak, became too unbearable, Nola unwrapped herself from him and scooted to the edge of the bed, pulling the blanket around her.

"Nola, don't. I'm sorry you went through all of that." Chase reached for her, but she moved farther away. "I'm just trying to process it all. I wish you had told me sooner."

"It's not something you blurt out in the middle of a conversation." Nola stood and pulled on her clothes, desperate to feel covered again. "I had no idea where this relationship was going or… It doesn't matter. It's obvious now. I can talk until I'm blue in the face and it won't change the way you feel."

"That's not fair. You don't know how I feel. I don't even know how I feel." Chase's tone softened as he tugged on his clothes. "I respect how personal this is for you, and I totally understand why you didn't tell me right away. Honey, I do. But why didn't you at least say you didn't want kids? You could have left out the details. You heard me going on this afternoon about how I want children. I want a house full of them, and you're telling me it's not possible with you. I'm trying to make sense of that. I wish you'd given me some idea so I could have made an informed decision before this went too far." As soon as the words were out of Chase's mouth, he wished he could take them back.

"You think we went too far?" Nola spun on him. "You stand there all high and mighty, giving me a load of crap, telling me you'll never hurt me. Here's a newsflash for you—you can't hurt me. No one can, ever again. Hurt is living with what I did. I ended my baby's life! I lost any chance of conceiving. Don't you get it? I don't deserve to be a mother. A woman lost her leg because of me. And do you know what she did? She asked the court for leniency on my behalf."

Nola squeezed her eyes shut and shook her head. "You once thanked me for my service in the Army, but the only reason I was there was because I had a brilliant attorney, thanks to good ol' Dad. It was his only gift to me. I was offered a choice—eight years in the service or five years in jail with a third-degree felony conviction. I chose the Army. It was familiar to me and I knew I could handle it. But it was the coward's way out. I deserved jail. I didn't even deserve the plastic surgery I had on my face, which is why I chose not to have any more. I killed my child. I maimed another human being. That's hurt. *You* can't hurt me."

Nola couldn't stand Chase staring at her for another second. She stormed into the bathroom and slammed the door behind her. She had known this wasn't going to end well. No matter how many times she had tried to convince herself that he would understand, that he would tell her it was okay and that he didn't judge her for what she'd done, she'd known that once she'd told Chase the truth it would be the end. Her whole relationship with Chase Langtry had been one big fat fantasy.

Nola heard her front door click shut. It was a sound she was familiar with—the sound of another door closing.

Chapter Ten

Chase was livid by the time he reached the ranch. Injury be damned, he needed to go for a ride. Lifting the saddle off the stand in the tack room sent a twinge of pain through his shoulder. Normally he'd ask one of the grooms to saddle Bocephus, but after Nola had called him high and mighty, Chase wanted to do it himself. Lord knew he'd saddled thousands of horses in his thirty years. There wasn't a job on this ranch that Chase hadn't done.

High atop his mount, Chase wound his way along one of the ranch's many trails. How could Nola presume to tell him how he felt? He wanted a family of his own and he'd thought he'd found the woman to share that with. He had envisioned it—Nola and his children, running around the ranch—as if it had been within his grasp. How could he have been so foolish? They hadn't known each other long enough for him to have any right to think that way.

Chase didn't want to hurt Nola, but he couldn't stay with her, either. And it clawed at his heart. He'd gotten involved too deep, too fast. If she had only told him before he'd invested in the relationship—before they'd slept together. He'd trusted her, bared his soul to her about his dreams and his fears. She could have told him then. Chase felt cheated. Nola had been the only woman he'd ever seen a future with, and now it was impossible.

The thunder of hooves sounded behind him. He turned to see Shane quickly closing the distance between them. "Go back to the stables," Chase called over his shoulder. "I don't want to talk about it."

"Okay." Shane made no move to leave.

"Suit yourself." Chase nudged Bocephus into a canter. A similar gait echoed behind him. Despite his protest, apparently Shane wasn't about to let him ride alone. When Chase reached a section of Cooter Creek that ran through their land, he slowed his horse to a walk. The December sun was warmer than normal, making his long-sleeved shirt feel stifling. Chase climbed down from the saddle and led Bocephus to the creek for a drink.

Removing his hat, Chase splashed water on his face in a vain attempt to cool down. Even with his body temperature lowered, his internal barometer was still off the charts. Shane continued to maintain a distance while remaining in sight.

"Why are you here?" Chase called down the creek to his brother.

"I didn't like the way you tore out of the stables. And with your shoulder I wanted to make sure you didn't fall."

"Bullshit." Chase rose and pulled his hat down low.

"We've all gone out on rides, injured, angry or both—we've never followed each other for protection."

"There's a difference between riding with an injury and riding with a broken heart." Shane led his horse toward Chase. "Remember when Jesse fell off his horse after that big blowup with Miranda?"

"How could I forget?" Chase thought back to the weeks immediately following his father's death. "That's when Miranda came back to him."

"I missed the majority of that because I was off somewhere being an ass, but thank God his injuries weren't as bad as they'd looked." Shane patted his horse's neck. "Chase, you've always wanted to be more involved in the family business, and it's commendable. If I ever made you feel like you had to choose something other than what you wanted for yourself, it wasn't my intention."

"You didn't." It was a rare occasion when Shane apologized for something. "For a while I thought I could be Superman and do it all, but I devoted the majority of my time to the rodeo, leaving the burden of the school and the ranch on the rest of you. In the end, I weighed what meant the most to me. As much as I love the rodeo, it was time to walk away. Something had to give and, while I always thought it would be my sanity, it turned out to be my shoulder. It was a blessing in disguise. It helped me make the decision I've been struggling with for a long time."

Shane knelt by the creek and cupped a handful of water. "Leaving the rodeo's like ending a relationship. For years, Lexi accused me of putting it before everything else…and she was right. Let me tell you, as much as you tend to shy away from the spotlight, you're going to miss it when it's gone."

"I'm sure I will." Chase dug his boots into the loose gravel along the creek. "At least when you retired, you had Lexi for support."

"Things over with Nola?"

"She can't have children." His brother didn't need to know the specifics. "Her timing for telling me really sucked."

"Ah." Shane caught his meaning. "There are other options available to you guys, you know. It doesn't mean you have to break up. Look at Tess and Cole. They adopted Ever and they're already talking about the possibility of adopting again."

"It doesn't even sound as if Nola wants to be a mother." Chase exhaled sharply. "I probably didn't handle it as well as I could have. I was shocked at the when and why."

Shane whistled. "That's tough. I know how much having a family means to you."

"Do you and Lexi ever talk about having another kid?"

Shane shook his head. "As much as I love Hunter, I'm still adjusting to the fact that he's mine. Don't get me wrong—I'm appreciative for every minute his adoptive parents have granted us, but some days it still doesn't feel real to me. I never saw myself having kids. I never wanted them until Dylan was born. Being there for the first year of his life, well, that's a feeling like no other you'll ever experience. And when I found out he wasn't mine... I don't wish that heartbreak on my worst enemy. Lexi and I came into this marriage with a ton of baggage, all of it my fault because of one mistake I made when I was eighteen. Lexi will carry the scars of giving up Hunter forever, and I will never forget Dylan. Emotionally, I don't think either one of us will ever be ready to have another child."

Shane had been the same age Nola was when her life had come to a crashing halt. Through his brother, Chase had witnessed firsthand how a mistake could eat away at your very existence, and he knew Nola had to be living with a similar pain. He was afraid his walking out on her earlier might have looked as if he was judging her for what had happened seven years ago, but it wasn't that at all.

"Maybe some time apart will do us good." A family of his own meant everything to him. He knew the available options. He loved his niece, Ever, as if she were his own flesh and blood. And he'd love another child if Tess and Cole decide to adopt again. "I don't know if I'm ready to give up the idea of having a child of my own for Nola."

"What does your heart tell you?" Shane asked.

"That our time together has been unlike any I've experienced with other women." But now Chase found himself questioning if his feelings for Nola had even been real. "And before you say it, I can't be in love with her."

Shane laughed. "Why not?"

"Love takes time." And he had looked forward to

that time with Nola, probably more than he was willing to admit to himself.

"I'll leave you with one piece of advice, even though you may not want to hear it." Shane swung himself into his saddle and nudged his horse away from the creek. "This morning's talk with Nola hurt, but so does falling off a horse for the first time. You need to realize where you went wrong, brush yourself off and do your best not to repeat the same mistake."

Mistake. Even now, Nola didn't feel like a mistake. She had fit perfectly—with him, with his life, with his family. Was it possible for him to get past the kid issue? Chase didn't think so. Why should he give up his dream when she wasn't even willing to discuss it?

"If you say the name Chase Langtry, I promise you they will be the last words you ever speak," Nola warned George as she climbed into the news van. Nola hated covering car accidents, but it was par for the course when you were an on-the-scene reporter. Just one more reason she wanted the co-anchor position.

"Whoa." George stilled Nola with his hand. "What happened to you?"

"I told Chase the truth about my past, that's what happened." Nola turned in the seat to face George. "I told him and he walked out on me. Prince Charming can go squat with his spurs on for all I care."

George laughed. "Since when does Prince Charming wear spurs?"

"Shut up and drive." Nola flipped open her iPad to

see if any other stations had arrived on scene yet. A calendar reminder blinked in the center of her screen. "Crap!"

"What's wrong?" George stopped the van at the edge of the parking lot.

"Keep driving." Nola waved her hand toward the street. "I completely forgot I have that studio interview with Kay tonight."

The last thing she wanted to do was face anyone from the Langtry clan. She was certain by now they all knew about her sordid past and they would never look at her the same way again. Breaking up with Chase was one thing, but their being disappointed in her as a human being was another.

"Kay's a good woman," George began. "I don't think she'll hold anything that happened between you and Chase against you personally."

"You can continue to live in fantasyland over there in your little corner of the world, but I'm through. I put too much faith into this whole thing with Chase and I got burned. Do you know he had the gall to tell me I should've told him I couldn't have kids sooner? Or at least said that I didn't want any. We've only been dating for a week. We were getting closer. Okay, we were as close as you could possibly get…physically. But still, the time wasn't right. Yesterday was the first day we were alone, without any interruptions from anyone."

"Allow me to play devil's advocate here." George steered the van onto the interstate. "If the relationship was so new and you've only been going out for a week, then why do you sound like it was more than some casual fling with possible future potential? Why are you so angry?"

Nola opened her mouth and then she snapped it shut. Reformulating her thought, she opened her mouth once again only to close it.

George looked in her direction. "Are you catching flies?"

"I don't have an answer." Nola sat looking out the passenger window. She couldn't explain why it bothered her so much.

"Need a little help?"

Nola scoffed. "You think you have the answer?"

"I believe you were not only falling in love with Chase. You were also falling in love with the life and family you never had. He was a package deal, and you knew that from the beginning whether you're willing to admit it to yourself or not."

Nola raised a brow at George's statement, her brain scrambling to find a logical argument against what he was saying. His words hammered in her head as they reached the scene. Nola fought to push them aside and focus on the tragedy unfolding in front of them.

"Park here." Nola flipped the sun visor down to check her reflection in the mirror. The woman staring back didn't begin to resemble the way she felt. Carefully applied makeup, hair styled with enough hairspray to shellac all fifty Miss America contestants and a red power suit designed to command attention successfully hid the shattered heart she had tried so carefully to protect.

Connecting her microphone to the battery pack as she walked toward the scene, George followed, his camera already hoisted into position filming the wreckage of the two-car accident. The paramedics had already arrived, and a body lay on the side of the road with a sheet draped over it.

Nola urged herself forward and quickly interviewed the people parked on the shoulder. Nodding to George when she had enough to report, Nola took a deep breath and assumed her position in front of the camera.

"This is Nola West reporting to you from the scene of a tragic accident this morning along I-10. Relatives of the victims tell me the couple and a group of their friends were on their way home to Ozona after attending a concert last night in San Antonio. Opting to leave this morning instead of making the three-hour drive in the dark, the caravan of cars ran into a patch of dense fog. There is one confirmed death and four people are on their way to area hospitals. Names of victims are being withheld at this time until families have been notified."

Nola stormed back to the van. "Send it to the studio. Let them edit it." She tossed her microphone into the back and tore off her battery pack. "I hate the news."

She climbed back into the van and slammed the door.

"Just because the Army said journalism was a good fit for you doesn't mean you have to make a career out of it." George closed the side door of the van and joined her up front. "What do you really want, Nola?"

"When I was growing up I dreamed of becoming a United Nations translator." Nola mused. "We'd lived in so many different countries, and the translators who accompanied us always amazed me. I loved studying foreign cultures and new languages. And the fact that I picked them up easily was one of the very reasons the Army thought being a public affairs broadcast specialist suited me."

When Nola had chosen the Army over jail, her dreams had ended. Basic training had been ten weeks of pure hell, but she'd reveled in it. It had kept her mind off what she'd done. Based on the results of her vocational aptitude battery, she'd followed boot camp with twelve weeks of advance individual training in the military occupation specialty they had assigned her based on her test results. Journalism hadn't been her choice. After she had come home on inactive duty, she'd enrolled in Texas A&M's telecommunications media studies program after receiving credit toward her bachelor's degree for her time in the Army. Her life hadn't turned out anything like she had planned.

"Nola, you're so young," George said. "You can go back to school and probably get your dream job before you're thirty. Don't waste the time you've been given. Listen to someone who's been there."

Nola sighed. "I've thought about it…many times." But once her life had started rolling in the journalism direction, she'd gone with it. She was good at her job and it had potential, but it just became one more empty goal for her to achieve. Her heart wasn't in it.

"Then, stop doing this to yourself."

"George, I appreciate the pep talk, but I can't worry about this now." Nola dialed the station to let them know they were leaving the scene and to check whether there were any other stories brewing before heading back to the office so she could prepare for her interview with Kay Langtry.

Nola wanted Kay to explain how the idea had come about and why it was so personal to her. Although she had originally agreed to cover the Mistletoe Rodeo to help defer Chase's loss in Las Vegas, that hadn't proved to be an issue once he had arrived back in Ramblewood. He was a hometown hero whose reputation and good name remained intact.

"We're clear—head back to the studio." When George didn't start the van, Nola looked through the windshield, trying to figure out why they weren't moving. "Is something blocking us?"

"Look at me," George demanded.

"What?" Nola overturned her palms. "I heard you before. I'll think about it, okay?"

"It's more than the job. You perpetually ignore what's right in front of you." George slapped the dashboard for emphasis. "You have a man in your life who truly cares about you. Okay, you can't have your own kids, but you can adopt. You can use a surrogate. You have so many options and you refuse to look at them because you've told yourself you don't deserve to have kids. I don't believe that crap for a second. And speaking of crap, you hate this job. Get your butt out there and do what you really want to do. Self-sabotage is what this is. You continuously punish yourself for something you did seven years ago. You did your time. Stop settling and start living."

Nola turned away, covering her mouth. George's words stung—stung because they were true. "I don't think I know how."

"THIS IS A SURPRISE." Cole turned on the remainder of the lights in the offices above the stables. "When did you get here?"

"I don't know." Chase was on his fifth cup of coffee and heartburn was beginning to set in. "I came up here to see if I could figure out something with this whole Scott David mess. If I stayed up at the house any longer, I would've had a Christmas meltdown. I swear Mom did twice as much this year as she did last year."

Cole pulled up a chair next to Chase at the conference table. "Did you come up with anything?" Cole sifted through the papers Chase had taken from Nola's condo yesterday. "You found all this?"

"No, Nola did. She first noticed Scott after I blew it in Vegas, but he's been gunning for us for a year."

"I didn't realize he'd gone after us publicly before now, or even to this extent." Cole removed his phone from his back pocket. "Jon said he didn't think Scott would do this, at least not yet anyway. I need to clue him in. I wish you'd told me yesterday."

"If I hadn't been so stubborn we would have

known about it the night Nola overheard us talking in Daddy's office. That's what she wanted to tell us."

"And then Jon made that comment about her being a reporter," Cole said.

Chase nodded. "Jon didn't trust Nola, and a part of me wondered if she was fishing for a story, as well."

Cole held up a finger for Chase to hold on. "Jon, it's Cole. When you get this, give me a call back on my cell. I have some information you may not be aware of regarding Scott David." Cole placed his phone on the table. "Is this all she has or is she able to dig up more information using her sources?"

Chase shrugged. "We broke up yesterday. I'm sure she won't want to be bothered helping us at all now."

"Doesn't Mom have that studio interview with her tonight?" Cole's brows furrowed. "Nola doesn't seem the type to blow off part of a story she's worked so hard for, but you may want to touch base with her. The Mistletoe Rodeo's your baby, too."

"I completely forgot about that interview." Chase didn't know whether he should call Nola or if his mother should. Technically, it was her interview, but he had planned to accompany her as cochair.

"For what it's worth, I'm sorry to hear about you and Nola. I hope you two can find a way to work out your differences, because you complement each other very well. I know Tess and Ever adore her."

"It's a complicated situation." Chase leaned back in his chair. "She confided in me and I could have reacted better. I've been wondering all night how to apologize."

"I can help you with that." Cole tore off a piece of paper and began to write on it. "Follow these instructions to the letter." Cole slid the paper across the table.

Chase looked down at the words: *Just say I'm sorry*.

"It's that simple, and Mom's interview is the perfect excuse," Cole said.

If only his relationship with Nola was that simple. They both wanted family, just not in the same way. In his vision of the future, he had always seen a little boy with his eyes or a little girl with his future wife's smile. Wasn't that everyone's dream? To have a miniature version of themselves running around? The resemblance between Shane and his son, Hunter, was remarkable. Chase wanted that so desperately for himself, but that desperation may have cost him the best thing that had ever happened to him.

NOLA SILENCED THE ringer on her phone. Chase had called three times since she'd been back in the office and hadn't left her a single voice mail. It couldn't possibly be about his mother's interview, because she'd already confirmed it with Kay.

Closing the door to her office, Nola rehearsed her questions. She rarely had the opportunity to interview somebody in the studio, and if it turned out well, she wanted to use it for a résumé reel.

George's words replayed in her head. Giving up her career was not an option. It wouldn't be practical to start over after all her training.

Children, however… She hadn't put much thought into adoption because of her criminal record. What adoption agency would give a woman who'd killed her unborn baby a child? Her only remote chance of being a parent was if she married someone who already had kids of their own. But then they would never truly be hers. And the surrogate option was definitely out of her financial reach.

But it wasn't out of Chase's.

Even if he was willing to discuss the possibility with her, the fact that he'd walked away after Nola had shared her deepest, darkest secret with him spoke volumes.

There was a knock on the door and George popped his head in. "I just wanted to check on you."

"Thanks, George—I'm fine. Be my guinea pig." It was always best to rehearse on a real person. "I need to make sure these questions are good enough for my interview with Kay."

George crossed the room and sat in front of Nola's desk. "I see you still have his flowers."

"They hovered over the garbage can twice this morning."

"Yet you decided to keep them. That says something." George tugged at the hem of his shirt where it had crept above his beer belly.

"The roses make my office smell nice." Nola waved her pen toward George's stomach. "You need to cut out the fast food."

"Nah, Betty must've shrunk this shirt in the wash." George wriggled in his chair. "Let's hear your questions."

By the time five o'clock rolled around, Nola was

primed and ready to go. Her producer let her know Kay had arrived and was waiting in their makeshift green room. He'd neglected to tell her that Chase was there with his mother.

Maintaining her composure, Nola acknowledged Chase with a brief lift of her chin and gave Kay a welcoming hug. If the woman knew anything about what had happened with Chase, she didn't let on.

"Don't be nervous." Nola felt the slight tremble in the woman's body. "The set itself will be lit, but the studio lights will be down low, so you'll hardly even see the cameras or the crew."

"Cameras?" Kay's gaze shifted from Nola to Chase and back again. "Multiple cameras?"

"There will be one behind you, one behind me and one straight ahead of us." Nola checked her watch. "Let's take a walk down there so you can get more of a feel for how this will work. The set resembles a plush living room."

Leading Kay down the hallway, Nola felt Chase's eyes sear into her back. After Kay saw where they would be conducting the interview, her nerves seemed more at ease. Nola's, however, had amped up a few notches thanks to Chase's presence.

As Nola reviewed the questions with Kay, Chase managed to squeeze in beside her despite her best efforts to keep a piece of furniture or other object between them.

"Can we talk afterward?" Chase asked when he could get a word in.

"Not if you're going to walk out on me again,"

Nola whispered, not wanting Kay to overhear their conversation. "I know I didn't exactly handle things perfectly, but still."

"How about I start with I'm sorry?" Chase's warm breath fell upon her neck.

"I think that would be a good starting point."

"Nola, phone call." One of the stagehands waved her over.

"Excuse me a moment. And yes, we can talk later." Nola looked toward Kay. "I'll be back in a minute. Just have a seat here."

Nola ran down the hallway to her office and picked up the phone. "Nola West speaking."

"Nola, it's Tommy over at the *Times*." Tommy was one of her go-to sources at the newspaper who always had her back when she needed it. "I just wanted to let you know that Scott David guy you asked me about came in here earlier making claims that your boyfriend's family stole his land. There was no way I could stop the story from running. It'll be in the online edition in an hour or so and they plan to run it as a front-page story in the morning."

"How can they do that without even speaking with the Langtrys? Why aren't they fact-checking? There's a lot more to this story than meets the eye."

"They've already sent a reporter over to their ranch. You may want to give them a heads-up."

"Thank you, Tommy." Nola squeezed her eyes tight as she hung up the phone. Her head began to throb.

"Nola, you're on in five."

What am I going to do? Mentally she ran through her list of options. She couldn't pull Kay from the interview. It was a live segment. She needed to give the woman a chance to defend her husband before the media ran wild with it. There was no time to warn her.

Nola's mouth went dry and a lump formed in her throat when she realized there was only one choice—Nola had to break the story first.

Chapter Eleven

Chase watched Nola arrive on set with only seconds to spare. A stagehand practically tripped over her as he clipped a microphone to her suit jacket.

Nola leaned toward Kay and whispered, "There's been a change. Just follow my lead and please trust me."

Panicked, Kay looked toward Chase standing off set. She clasped her hands tightly in front of her as the floor manager counted them down. And she began.

"Hello, I'm Nola West, here today with Kay Langtry of the Bridle Dance Ranch in Ramblewood. Welcome to our show."

"Thank you for having me," Kay said.

"For the viewers who aren't already familiar with the Langtry family, Bridle Dance is one of the state's largest paint and quarter cutting horse ranches, in addition to a winery and a sod farm. Two years ago, Kay, your sons opened the Ride 'em High! Rodeo School and you are the CEO of the Dance of Hope Hippotherapy Center. Can you tell me a bit about Dance of Hope?"

"Hippotherapy utilizes a horse's movements to treat people with various injuries and disabilities. Dance of Hope is a nonprofit organization that welcomes everyone—nobody is ever turned away because of their inability to pay. We have guest cottages where families can stay while their loved ones go through therapy. Many members of our staff reside on the ranch, so there is always somebody there to provide the best possible care."

Chase had to hand it to his mother. As nervous as she was on the inside, she appeared confident throughout her responses. He wondered why Nola had led off with that particular line of questioning.

"Your initial investment in Dance of Hope came from your own pocket, is that correct?" Chase furrowed his brow; Dance of Hope's finances had nothing to do with the Mistletoe Rodeo.

"Bridle Dance funded a large portion of it and I added to it."

"Let's talk about your husband, Joe Langtry. You've said during previous interviews that Dance of Hope was his vision before he died three and a half years ago."

At Nola's mention of his father, a bad feeling developed in the pit of Chase's stomach.

"It was. He originally became interested in hippotherapy through our granddaughter, Ever."

"Ever is the little girl your son Cole and his wife adopted. She has cerebral palsy, correct?" Nola nodded her head slowly, encouraging Kay to answer.

The smile plastered across Kay's face had begun

to falter as Nola revealed more personal information than was necessary. It was no secret that Ever had been adopted or that she had cerebral palsy, but this was not the time or place to discuss it.

"Yes. But I don't see—"

"Let's talk about the acreage your family has purchased over the years. Your husband acquired a large portion of it because your neighbors were facing foreclosure and Joe stepped in, offering them much higher than market value for their property so they wouldn't walk away with nothing."

No! No! No! Chase knew where Nola was heading and he was furious. "Mom, don't."

"He—he did." If she'd heard her son, Kay didn't acknowledge it. "And he leased it back to them if they still wanted to farm or ranch on it."

Kay exhaled slowly, maintaining steady eye contact with Nola. Chase wasn't sure if his mother was trying to get a read on Nola or if she was trying to frighten her, but either way, it wasn't a good look and it definitely came across on the monitor.

"Joe Langtry was a very generous man," Nola continued. "Known for his charitable contributions throughout the state, not just in Ramblewood. How do you feel when you hear that there's a man out there making claims that your husband stole mineral rights from his grandfather?"

Oh, no she didn't.

Chase watched his mother's face begin to redden. "I think it's a bunch of bunk," Kay said matter-of-factly. "The man in question was in competition with my husband for two decades. He still has a bug up him because my Joe outbid him on numerous land acquisitions over the years."

"Over the past year this person has made frequent personal attacks online targeting your family and has increased them this week. What are your thoughts on that?"

"I didn't know about that. Scott David—let's just call him by his name, shall we—tried to fleece my family for a hundred million dollars this past weekend with these ridiculous claims of his, but he didn't get his way. Scott David is nothing more than someone with an ax to grind because he couldn't get the land he wanted. He claims his grandfather had Alzheimer's when he sold the mineral rights to his land to my husband. I don't see how any attorney in the world would have allowed their client to sign away such a significant thing as mineral rights if he wasn't of sound mind and body."

Chase's cell phone vibrated in his pocket. Jon's number appeared on the screen. No sooner had he answered than he heard Jon screaming, "Get her off camera now!"

Chase motioned to Nola to end the interview, slicing his hand back and forth in front of his neck. But she continued to question his mother. When Chase attempted to step on set, one of the stagehands grabbed his arm and pulled him back.

"Let go of me!" Chase shouted, shoving the man backward into one of the cameras. Nola and Kay both stood on seeing the commotion. "This interview is over." Chase locked eyes with Nola. "And so are we."

"IT'S NOT WHAT you think," Nola tried to explain as she followed Chase through the studio hallways, making his way to the parking lot with Kay. "I had to do it. Please stop—you need to listen to me. This is going to be front-page news tomorrow morning and there's a reporter on the way to your house."

"Only because you made it that way!" Chase shouted over his shoulder. "You either stay away from me and my family or I'll have a restraining order issued against you so fast your head will spin. And don't think I can't do it."

Nola stood motionless at the cruelty of Chase's words. After his SUV drove away, she trudged back through the studio's entrance, removing her microphone and throwing it in the trash outside her office as she walked by. She opened her desk drawer and removed her handbag and keys.

"Nola!" Pete Devereaux burst into the room. "Amazing work. That is exactly the hard-hitting story I was looking for from you. I knew you could do it. I think I've made my decision on the co-anchor position."

"Give it to Dirk." Nola squeezed past him. "Because I quit."

"What?" Pete followed her out of the office. "Nola, come on. I know he was your boyfriend and all, but you can't mix love and war. The news is war."

Nola spun on Pete, stopping inches from his face.

"Don't you dare talk to me about war. I've been there. While you were sitting here in your cushy air-conditioned office, I was trying to escape enemy shellfire. You don't know anything."

She turned and continued walking. "You're making a big mistake!" Pete shouted after her.

That might be so, but at least she'd still have her dignity.

Nola pulled out of the parking lot, refusing to cry. She had more self-worth than that. She needed to get to the Langtrys and explain what had happened. She knew Chase wouldn't listen to her—he'd probably even throw her off the ranch—but she had to try something.

She pulled off to the side of the road and dug through her bag for her phone. The moment she found it, Kylie's number appeared on the screen. "I was just about to call you."

"What is going on?" Kylie's voice was frantic. "Jesse is furious."

"Jesse? How would you know Jesse was mad?"

"Aaron works for Miranda and Jesse. We were over at their house watching the interview. Jesse flew out of there and I don't know if he's heading to the ranch or if he's looking for you. But he's furious, Nola. You can't go home."

"I hope he does find me," Nola said. "Then, maybe someone will listen. I need your help. Minutes before we went live, I received a phone call from one of my sources. He said Scott David had already told his side of the story and this stolen-mineral-rights thing was going to be all over the internet in an hour—more like a half hour now. It'll be front-page news tomorrow. I had no choice but to allow Kay to set the record straight before the media destroyed the Langtry name. I was trying to protect them."

"Where are you right now?" Kylie asked.

"Parked at the side of the road. Maybe I'll go home and see if I can intercept Jesse."

"No, meet me at my house. Aaron and I will be there shortly."

Nola started her car and continued on toward Ramblewood. When she pulled into her aunt and uncle's driveway, they were waiting for her on the front porch. They ushered her inside, offering her a shoulder to cry on if she needed one.

"I'm fine, Aunt Jean." Nola sat on the edge of the couch and accepted the scotch on the rocks her uncle handed her. Swirling the amber liquid in the glass, Nola tried to figure out her next maneuver.

"You remind me so much of your father when you have that look on your face," Dan said.

"Lieutenant General August West." Nola tried to remember when she had last seen her father smile, realizing she didn't think she ever had. "He's a hard man. I hope I'm not too much like him."

"You have his strength and determination." Dan smiled. "That's where the similarities end. Although you do look a little like him around the eyes. At least in his younger days."

"Was the military always my father's dream?"

"Your father wanted to be a pilot. That's all he

talked about growing up, and when he went into the Army, that's what he thought he would become. But his vision wasn't good enough. He certainly made the best of it, though. He's done very well for himself and he's proud of that."

"Pride comes at a price," Nola said. "I missed so much of my childhood. I hadn't even realized it until I started spending time with the Langtrys and saw how things are supposed to be. I'm not saying their life is like everybody else's, but I've learned that our home was not normal. Now that I've had a taste of it, I don't want to let go. Everything I did today was to protect the Langtrys."

"We know that, honey," her aunt reassured.

Kylie and Aaron arrived a few minutes later and Nola explained to the four of them the events leading up to Kay's TV appearance.

"Kay said things during that interview that Chase hadn't mentioned to me before. I don't know if he chose not to tell me or if he just didn't know. I need to clear my name with them. There has to be some way for me to make them understand. Chase even threatened me with a restraining order. Do you know how that makes me feel?"

"If any man ever threatened me with a restraining order, that would be the last time he ever saw me." Kylie turned her head toward Aaron.

"What are you looking at me for?" Aaron gave his fiancée a kiss on the cheek.

"I know you have strong feelings for Chase, and because I know him so well, I'll give him a pass this time, but only this once." Kylie turned toward Aaron again. "Do you think you could talk to Jesse and get him to see things from Nola's perspective?"

"Sure," Aaron agreed. "Although I think Miranda is my better bet. She was attempting to calm Jesse down. I think she realized there was more going on than what we saw on television."

Nola slumped against the back of the couch. If Miranda had suspected something was up, then maybe Kay had, too. Nola hoped she'd given Kay enough body signals to let her know she wasn't purposely being malicious.

"Something about Scott David keeps nagging at me and I can't put my finger on it. I've followed every lead I could think of and things just don't add up. My sources told me Scott hadn't spoken to his grandfather in over twenty years. It was only when Nate David went into a nursing home that Scott showed any interest in the man. That leads me to believe the issue was financial all along, but Scott's net worth is a million times more than Nate's. I can't get the puzzle pieces to fit together, and I feel like the Langtrys are running out of time. With the Mistletoe Rodeo in a few days, they can't afford to have their name dragged through the mud. If that event fails, the people who are in such desperate need of the food bank's assistance will be the ones who suffer the most."

"I know someone who can help," Aaron said. "I'm sure if we go there right now, he'll do whatever he can."

"We all will." Jean took Nola's hands in hers. "I

know we haven't spent a lot of time together over the years, but we'll do anything to help you."

Nola wished she had made more of an effort with her aunt and uncle before now. They were supporting her despite the distance she'd maintained, and she was glad.

Nola actually did have a family, one she could count on.

AFTER KAY'S DISASTROUS INTERVIEW, the entire Langtry family met back at the ranch. Chase was so mad at Nola, he had difficulty seeing straight. If this was her idea of revenge for the way he'd treated her at her condo, then he wanted nothing to do with her.

"How much damage did that do to us?" Cole asked.

Jon perused his iPad before setting it down. "Actually, Nola may have done you a favor."

"She broke a scandal about our father on the six o'clock news and you think she did us a favor?" Shane spat. "It's all over the internet already."

"Have you actually read what's online?" Jon scanned the room. "Because I have, and what's there doesn't match what Nola said in her interview. Actually, Nola didn't say much about Scott David at all—it was Kay who let the details out of the bag. I don't know if that was clever planning on Nola's part to get Kay to divulge information, or if she genuinely didn't know as much as she thought she did."

Chase fumed. Regardless of what she knew, the interview should have been about the Mistletoe Rodeo.

Instead, Nola had used his family so she could advance her career. He hoped it was worth it to her.

"This was coming out whether we wanted it to or not," Jon continued. "The timestamps on the online articles are minutes after Nola's interview. There's too much additional information in there for the interview to have triggered those articles."

"You think somebody had already leaked the story?" Cole asked.

"I do." Jon rubbed the back of his neck. "I think it was Scott David. The *Times* is reporting an exclusive."

"When Nola ran into the studio before the interview, she was visibly upset," Kay said. "She asked me to follow her lead and trust her. I'm sorry if some of you don't agree, but in my heart of hearts, I know she was trying to tell me something. Something had happened—"

"Mom?" Cole asked. "What is it?"

"Something did happen." Kay looked at Chase. He hadn't noticed the dark circles under his mother's eyes until then and they concerned him. "Nola had a phone call."

She was right. That was why Nola had left the room moments before the interview. "When she didn't return right away, her producer began to panic," Chase added.

Kay's shoulders straightened. "When she came back, her whole demeanor had changed."

"That's interesting. She may have been tipped off that the story was about to break," Jon said. "In the meantime, if anyone asks you anything, say no comment. There's security in place at all the ranch entrances, and the one reporter who did manage to get in has been removed."

Feeling claustrophobic, Chase stepped out onto the back porch overlooking the ranch—the legacy of his father, grandfather and great-grandfather. How could one man, a stranger to most of them, viciously attack his father's name? Even if there was the slightest bit of truth to his story, he could at least have the decency to speak to the family directly. Threatening and demanding exorbitant amounts of money made Scott David a coward in his book.

Furthermore, he could have saved his attack on the family until after the Mistletoe Rodeo. Chase hadn't expected to get so attached to the project, but now he wondered if all their efforts had been for naught. One of the biggest draws to the event was his family's name. If people suspected the Langtrys of illegal business dealings, the whole thing might fall apart.

As for Nola, she was his problem. He had brought her into his family and he was prepared to pay for the repercussions. He had gained full access to his trust fund on his birthday and he would personally replenish any food bank funding the Mistletoe Rodeo lost. Chase refused to allow anyone's Christmas to suffer because of his actions. Too many people deserved the community's help, and Chase would be damned if he'd stand by and let anyone take it away from them.

"Oh, no!" Nola, Kylie and Aaron stood on Clay Tanner's front step. "You're not welcome here."

"Clay." Aaron wedged himself between Nola and the closing door. "I'm asking you as a friend to listen to what Nola has to say. Once you do, I promise you won't turn her away."

"Let them in, Clay." A woman's voice came from the other side of the door.

Clay stepped aside and they filed into his living room.

"Hi, Nola." The woman who spoke was blonde and very petite. "I'm Abby, Clay's wife. Please pardon his manners. We would've met at the cookie party, but I was on my way back from Charleston that night and couldn't get there in time. I'm sorry I missed it." Abby turned toward Aaron and Kylie and gave them a group hug. "I know I can't tell you two enough, but I am over-the-moon happy for you both."

Abby might be friendly, but her husband was shooting Nola death rays with his eyes from across the room. Two more people walked out of the kitchen to join them.

"I don't know if you've met or not. This is my twin sister, Bridgett, and her husband, Adam," Abby said.

Twin sister? That was unexpected. At least a foot in height separated the two women. "Actually, I've known Bridgett for a few years," Nola said. "You used to wait tables at The Magpie."

"What brings you by?" Tight, thin lips replaced Bridgett's usual smile. Warmth had definitely taken a vacation.

"I'm assuming you've all seen the news." Aaron stood in the middle of the room playing referee. "I'm asking you to listen to what Nola has to say. And, Clay, as a friend of the Langtrys and the best private investigator I know, we need your help."

Nola told her story once again. By the time she had finished, Clay was hanging on every word. Believing she wanted to help the Langtrys, he broke protocol and filled her in on what she didn't already know.

"I want to see Nate David," Nola said. "If he has at least some coherency, then maybe he can tell me something about the day in question. Maybe even the name of a friend who could vouch for him at the time. There's quite a gap between the time Scott says Nate developed Alzheimer's and when he actually went into the nursing home."

"I want to know who's been visiting him," Clay added. "Whoever's dropping in on him now may have been around back then. But, Nola, you can't go there. The risk of somebody recognizing you from television is too great, even all the way up there."

"I'll do it." Abby stood and removed her HC General credentials from her handbag. "I work at Dance of Hope, but I'm also a physical therapist for the hospital here. I have the perfect cover."

Clay sighed and rolled his eyes. "I have to admit you would fit rather nicely into this investigation."

"Finally!" Abby clapped her hands together. "I've been asking to assist him for over a year now. He always says no."

"Do you really think Joe Langtry is innocent?"

Bridgett asked Clay. "You knew him better than any of us."

Clay seemed to weigh his words. "To people on the outside looking in, Joe could seem ruthless at times. He was a very shrewd businessman, and I can't see him doing something that had the potential to come back and bite him. He had the money to make sure anything he did was legal, and he didn't make mistakes in business. I don't know if Scott David truly believes Joe did his grandfather wrong or if this is a revenge thing. Either way, I agree with Nola. We need to figure it out before the Mistletoe Rodeo."

"I want you all to know how much I appreciate your help." Nola had definitely learned a lesson in small-town camaraderie today. "I'm grateful for the second chance to make things right with the Langtrys."

Bridgett and Adam laughed quietly together. "I'm sorry. We're not laughing at you," Bridgett said. "We're laughing at what you said. A lot has happened around here over the past couple years and second chances have been handed out as if they were going out of style. Adam has even had a few of his own."

If they could save the Mistletoe Rodeo, then maybe Chase would be willing to give her a second chance, too. Nola knew the man needed space, but she couldn't just let him believe that she had betrayed his family.

"I'm going to head to Miranda and Jesse's now." Aaron stood and stretched his arms over his head. "I think we have a long night ahead of us. I'll give you guys a call as soon as I know something."

Kylie kissed her fiancé goodbye. Nola already missed the easy companionship she had shared with Chase. As quickly as it had come, it had gone. It shouldn't matter. It was crazy for her to be this worked up over a man.

A part of her hated Chase for letting her down. He'd taught her how to feel again. He'd given her hope and had made it okay to enjoy the spirit of Christmas. Now when she went home, she'd have to face the gingerbread house and the Christmas tree and sleep in a bed they had recently shared.

The same bed where Chase had broken her heart. Nola's condo had always been her safe zone. She had kept it devoid of memories and had never allowed anyone she dated inside. Why hadn't she stopped Chase at the door?

Because he felt like home.

Chapter Twelve

The morning of the Mistletoe Rodeo was bedlam around the Langtry house. Kay ran in overdrive, barking orders so fast Chase was worn out before the sun came up.

The entire Langtry clan gathered in the kitchen, poring over the day's agenda. Lexi was in charge of the tricky tray raffle at the firehouse, Tess was hosting the Christmas carol pancake brunch at the Methodist Church, Chase and Kay were the masters of ceremonies for the Mistletoe Rodeo itself and Miranda was hosting the charity dinner and auction in the new Ramblewood Food Bank addition. Shane, Jesse and Cole were in charge of anything with four legs at the fairgrounds, and the rest of the extended family was running everything in between.

A caravan of forty vehicles and trailers rolled out of Bridle Dance by six o'clock, everyone heading off in separate directions. All of the hard work had come down to this one day, and Chase wanted nothing more than to have Nola by his side to share the joy.

It turned out their attorney had been right about

Nola's interview—they all owed her a huge thank-you. By covering the story first, she had allowed Kay to preempt Scott David before he did too much damage. A few Mistletoe Rodeo sponsors had pulled out, but Chase had found replacements easily enough. The legal battle with Scott was far from over, but thanks to a gag order, no one involved could publically discuss the case.

Five days had passed since Nola's interview. Chase had driven out to her condo in Willow Tree on three occasions, and either she wouldn't answer the door or she legitimately wasn't home, even though her Beetle was in the parking lot. Chase chose to believe she had been out wedding shopping with Kylie, but a part of him sensed she had chosen to stay away. And he couldn't blame her.

When George had called and told him Nola had quit her job even after she'd been offered the co-anchor position, Chase's heart broke. If he'd never gotten involved with her, she'd still have a job. He knew it was her choice to leave, but he felt partially to blame.

Chase understood that Nola had been trying to protect his family during her final interview. Maybe someday he'd get the chance to apologize. He could've made it easier on himself and called her, but it felt too impersonal. They needed to talk face-to-face. As for his decision about dating Nola, it hadn't changed. He wished he could say it had. A family of his own was too important for him to walk away from, and unless Nola could meet him halfway, it would never work.

Chase pulled into the fairgrounds behind Shane.

With their bulls and broncs, the Ride 'em High! Rodeo School was ready to put on a great exhibition rodeo. Many of his students were competing, including Hunter, who was staying in Ramblewood during the Christmas break.

"Woo-hoo! Ride 'em high, brother," Shane shouted. He was in rare form this morning, no doubt reliving his own rodeo days through his son.

Chase wandered into the middle of the arena and looked up toward the bleachers, all decked out in Christmas trim. The brides of Bridle Dance had taken over and run amok last night, decorating one location after the other. He'd never seen so much crepe paper in his life, yet rarely had he felt less festive.

NOLA HAD BEEN up all night staring at the same stacks of paper on her dining room table. With the gag order in place, there was no longer a rush to solve the Scott David mystery. But it was the principle of the thing. She'd lost everything because a stranger attacked the family she'd grown to love. Now she was determined to take him down along with her. She had nothing left to lose.

The good news was that Clay and Abby's nursing home mission had been a wild success, albeit a slightly illegal one. When they had discovered Nate David wasn't able to remember much of his life, let alone the sale of the mineral rights, Clay had taken drastic measures.

While Abby had occupied the nurses' station, Clay had managed to slip the visitor registry book into the bathroom, photographed all the pages with his phone and put it back into place with no one being the wiser. Nola and Clay had each taken half the list. There were a few people who regularly visited Nate, and Nola had left messages for each of them to call her back. Every person except for one woman had returned her call. Nola hoped that person held the answers and would agree to testify against Scott, because none of the others would. Either they didn't want to get involved or they hadn't known Nate at the time of the sale.

Nola felt Flash rub against her leg. She reached down and scratched her pure-black feline friend between the ears. The night she returned home from Clay's she'd thrown the gingerbread house down the garbage shoot along with the sheets from her bed, and had given the Christmas tree to her next-door neighbor. It had been cathartic. She'd needed to remove all traces of Chase from her home.

The following day, since she'd had an excessive amount of time on her hands, she had purchased new bedding and a couple cans of paint. Then she had adopted Flash from the local animal shelter. Now she had deep cherry-red bedroom walls and a sunny yellow living area, and she was no longer alone.

She'd also taken the time to call her parents in the Netherlands. After an hour-long conversation with her mother, followed by a phone call to her brother, she'd managed to convince her family to attempt a visit to Ramblewood for Kylie's spring wedding. At the very least, her mother had promised to come, even if her brother and father couldn't get away.

Checking her watch, Nola realized she needed to get ready if she planned on making the tricky tray on time. She hadn't been to one of those in years, and today she was determined to win something. A TV would be nice—her twenty-inch set was beyond pathetic.

Today would be the first day she'd see the Langtrys since the interview. The one day she'd been brave enough to visit Kay, she'd been turned away at the main gate. Employees, family and scheduled visitors were the only ones allowed on the ranch nowadays. But Kay had taken the time to phone and thank her for all she'd done to help them.

Nola began to have second thoughts as she pulled up to the Ramblewood firehouse an hour later. When Kylie and her mother parked next to Nola a few seconds later, the reality of facing all the friends and family she had humiliated began to set in, despite Kay's call. But Kylie had invited her and Nola was prepared to see it through.

Kylie walked over and opened the driver's side door of Nola's Beetle and pulled her to her feet.

"You'll be just fine." Kylie and Jean linked arms with her, one on either side, propelling her toward the entrance. When they walked in, the boisterous room fell silent.

For a few seconds.

Then went back to boisterous again.

The three women purchased a hundred dollars' worth of tickets each and skimmed the list of prizes on the wall.

"Nola!" Lexi greeted her with a hug. "It's wonderful to see you. I know Kay spoke to you already, but I do hope you realize how grateful we are for what you did with that interview. You really saved the day by taking a potentially disastrous situation and making it less volatile."

"It was nothing." Nola searched the room for—no, not Chase. Chase wouldn't be at a tricky tray.

"He's at the fairgrounds, if you're interested." Lexi placed a hand on her forearm. "If it's any consolation, he's been miserable without you."

Nola's heart thudded against her chest at the news. It was a consolation. A very good one. She wanted Chase to miss her. Maybe there was a slight glimmer of hope in all of this.

"Lexi, do you have any idea where the extra tickets are?" Kay's normally calm demeanor looked as if it had been struck by lightning. "Nola, hello." Kay leaned in and gave her a quick peck on the cheek. "I'm delighted you could make it. Chase is over at the fairgrounds if you want to stop by and see him."

Nola pursed her lips. "Lexi already covered that one."

"Yeah," Lexi said, "I did, but she wouldn't take the bait."

"Extra tickets?" Kay frowned at Lexi.

"I'm sorry. I'll get them now." Lexi tore off toward the back of the room, waving goodbye over her shoulder.

"We won't keep you," Kylie gracefully interjected, pulling Nola from an awkward moment.

"Don't be a stranger," Kay said before dashing off toward another minicrisis.

"That sounded promising." Kylie linked her arm in Nola's as they walked the perimeter of the room, trying to decide which bowls to choose for their raffle tickets.

"Do you really think so?" Nola hated sounding anxious, but she did want to see Chase.

"Oh, please." Kylie shook her head. "And people call *me* an airhead. Where on earth did my mom go?"

"She's over there." Nola pointed to the far corner of the room, and that was when she saw it. She dragged Kylie with her to stand in front of a large seventy-five-inch television. "This one. This is the one I want." Nola tore off her tickets one by one and tossed them into the aquarium-size bowl.

"There must be a couple thousand tickets in there already." Kylie laughed. "Good luck."

This was her lucky day. She could feel it. The Langtrys—some of them, at least—had forgiven her. And as soon as the tricky tray was done, she'd head over to the fairgrounds to see if Chase had, too.

"Lexi called. Nola's over at the tricky tray," Shane called to Chase as he made another pass with the arena drag, loosening the soil and ensuring it was level.

Chase was surprised she'd come when she knew he would be there. Not that he would go to the tricky tray. Although, if one wanted to support his mother's charity work, especially if one was cochair, one really should take the time to put in an appearance at all of the day's events.

"I'll be back in a few," Chase shouted over the noise of the tractor. "I'm going to check in on Mom."

"Sure you are," Shane shouted back. "Tell Nola I said hello."

Between the traffic and the long lines of cars waiting to get into the center of Ramblewood, the tricky tray was over by the time Chase arrived at the firehouse and Nola was nowhere to be found. Heading off to the Methodist Church for the pancake brunch, Chase reasoned he could grab a bite, just to make sure the pancakes were edible. If he happened to run into Nola it would be nothing more than a coincidence.

Fighting the traffic back across town, Chase began to wonder if it would have been faster to walk. He finally made it and found a parking spot. As he walked in the side door, he saw his mother, Lexi and Tess making their rounds to all of the tables, thanking everyone for coming. *What a great idea.*

Chase approached the first table, quickly scanning it for Nola. "Merry Christmas. Thank you for coming." Chase shook hands as he walked to the next table over. "Merry Christmas, and thank you for supporting the Ramblewood Food Bank."

After ten tables, he was tired of shaking hands and still hadn't spotted Nola or anyone from her family. He passed his mother greeting the next row over, and she smiled appreciatively at him.

"I'm so glad you made it, honey," Kay said before moving on to another table.

As Chase shook the final hand at the last table in the room, he couldn't help but feel a stab of disappointment. He passed right by the kitchen on his way toward the exit, no longer hungry.

"Hey, Chase." Lexi backed out the kitchen door with two trays full of pancakes. "Can you take one of these? Who knew pancakes were so heavy?"

"Sure." Chase eased a tray out of her arms.

"They go to this row. You take the outside, I'll take the inside." Lexi placed a steaming stack of pancakes on the serving table every two feet. "Did you hear Nola won that huge TV at the tricky tray?"

Chase's head shot up at the sound of her name. "No, I hadn't heard." He smiled. He served the last plate of pancakes on his tray and followed Lexi back toward the kitchen.

"You should have seen it." Lexi started laughing. "Nola, Jean and Kylie attempting to squeeze that big television into Nola's tiny car. Dan had to come pick it up in his truck. I hope they get back before we run out of food."

As happy as he was for Nola, he was disappointed that he'd missed her. Why did it even matter? He had been resolute in his decision about having children. Nothing had happened to make him think she'd changed her mind. But something had changed... He had.

"I CAN'T BELIEVE I won this thing." Nola said as they tugged it out of the box. "It's huge."

"It takes up a good portion of your living room."

Kylie tilted her head back. "If you sit on the couch and watch it, it'll be like sitting in the front row at the movies."

"Uncle Dan, you don't need to set it up for me." Nola felt bad enough about dragging everyone away from the Mistletoe Rodeo to help her get her TV home. "I'll do it later. Since we missed the pancake brunch, how about I treat you all to breakfast and then we'll make our way over to the rodeo?"

"How about I treat, since you're unemployed." Nola's uncle gave her one of his stern "I won't take no for an answer" looks.

"I have money." Nola locked up behind them as they left the condo. "It's not as if I've splurged much since I moved here. My savings can potentially hold me over for a few years. But I will not turn down a free breakfast."

Nola wasn't sure if her relationship with her parents would ever be repaired, but she felt as if they were off to a good start. Having her aunt and uncle in her life had helped to fill that void. Regardless of how things turned out with Chase, she'd be forever in his debt for showing her what Christmas meant. It wasn't about the decorations or the presents. It was about spending time with family and embracing the love around her instead of hiding from it.

"Let's go, everyone—I'm starving." Nola's phone fell out of her bag as she unlocked her car door. She picked it up and noticed a message from a number she didn't recognize. She held up one finger, asking her family to wait while she checked her voice mail.

Her heart began to pound rapidly as she listened to the message. "There is a Santa Claus!"

"Who was that?" Jean asked.

"I think I just found the missing link to clear Joe Langtry's name once and for all." Nola had struck pay dirt. "I need to call this woman back. Go on to breakfast without me. And please don't say anything to anyone about this. I need to be sure before I get the Langtrys' hopes up."

Her family gave her a group hug before they left, a gesture that was starting to feel very natural to Nola. Dialing the woman's number, Nola silently prayed this was the answer they'd been searching for.

"Jennifer, this is Nola West. Thank you for calling me back."

CHASE DIDN'T APPRECIATE having to wear an elf costume in the rodeo arena. "Why does Cole get to be Santa Claus and I'm an elf?"

"Because Cole's the oldest," Tess huffed. "Now put on your ears and your pointy toes and quit belly-aching. You have an ostrich to ride."

"Great." Chase flopped down on the bench. Being relegated to riding a big bird dressed as an elf in a Christmas show was a far cry from his rodeo days. "Thanks."

"Look at me." Abby lifted his chin. "The doctor didn't clear you to ride a bronc or a bull. As your physical therapist, it's my job to keep an eye on you. You were given the okay to ride an ostrich. It doesn't buck, it's closer to the ground and all you need to do is sit down, shut up and hang on. I have faith in you, Grumpy Elf."

"Wasn't Grumpy a dwarf?" Chase asked.

"In your case, he's an ostrich-riding elf."

Chase didn't even want to look at himself in the mirror before he strode out of the makeshift dressing room. "Where is my fine feathered friend anyway?"

"They're on the way." Shane flipped through the pages on his clipboard. "They hit some traffic on the interstate—not the birds themselves, you know what I mean—and we're figuring at least an hour more. I'm going to move Hunter's division up and that should buy us some time."

Chase shook his head, the bell on the tip of his hat jingling. "I have to wear this thing for an hour?"

"Sorry." Shane shrugged. "You have to admit, it is kind of funny. Since you're dressed for it, why don't you go rile up the crowd while I get things together?"

"You're kidding, right?"

"No, Chase, I'm not." Shane started to laugh. "I'm sorry. I can't get mad at you when you're dressed like that. You owe me anyway for skipping out for two hours this morning."

"I got held up at the brunch. Your wife put me to work."

"Well, now I'm putting you to work. Cochairs have to get dirty, too."

Luckily for Chase, the ostriches arrived a short time later, and after a quick refresher course—he hadn't ridden one since he was sixteen—Chase felt a little more secure and less like—what? An elf riding an ostrich?

"Who's my opponent?" Chase glanced around the holding area.

"I am, and don't you dare say a word." Lexi climbed up and over the fence wearing a ridiculous red and gold elf suit. Abby and Tess must have had to hog-tie her in order to get the false eyelashes and inordinate amount of blush on her cheeks. "My husband is so dead for this."

"At least you make me feel better about myself." Chase laughed.

"Come on, you—" Cole took one look at the two of them together and then looked away. "There are no words. Follow me."

In the center of the arena, the ostrich handlers helped Chase and Lexi mount the birds within the confines of the corral. Firmly seated on its back, Chase gripped the bird's wings and leaned back. He squeezed his legs around the ostrich's midsection, and the gate swung open.

Oh, hell!

NOLA HAD RUN from one end of the fairgrounds to the other and she still hadn't found Chase or any of the Langtry brothers. Hearing cheers from within the arena, Nola showed her Mistletoe Rodeo all-events wristband at the gate and walked down the corridor between the bleachers.

Then she saw them: Lexi and Chase, dressed as the world's most deranged-looking elves racing each other across the arena on ostriches. She whipped out her phone and quickly began to record the spectacle.

This will look amazing on my new television.

Lexi won the race, and in her excitement, she waved her arms in the air, promptly falling backward off her ostrich. Seeing Lexi on the ground, Chase's ostrich stopped short, sending him up and over his bird's head.

"Oh, my God!" Nola's hand flew to her chest. She ran to the fence rails for a better view, only to find Lexi and Chase laughing hysterically in the dirt.

"Ladies and gentlemen." Shane walked into the arena dressed as Santa Claus with a microphone in hand. "Please give our two riders a hand. My brother Chase and my wife, Lexi."

The crowd applauded. Nola watched Chase help Lexi up and then say something in her ear. She nodded and then both elves took off running after Santa. Poor Shane was at a disadvantage with oversize black boots on and a belly full of stuffing getting in the way.

When they caught him, they called out for help. Hunter, Cole and Jesse ran into the ring. The five of them carried Shane back over to the ostrich corral while a wrangler made sure one was in position. Lifting him up onto the bird, they sent Shane on a ride of his own. To his credit, he stayed on longer than either Chase or Lexi had.

The crowd loved it and if Nola didn't know better, she'd have thought they'd rehearsed the whole thing earlier. Nola waved to Chase but he turned away before he saw her, heading toward the Junior Rodeo crowd. There wasn't any way she'd be able to talk to him now. Her news would have to wait until the charity dinner and auction.

CHASE STOOD BESIDE his mother and brothers at the entrance to the newly constructed Ramblewood Food Bank addition. After a touching speech by Evelyn Koch, Kay held the ribbon up as Evelyn wielded a giant pair of scissors and cut it in half.

The doors swung wide to reveal a large open room with a vaulted oak beamed ceiling. Rows of tables elegantly draped in red and white linens created a dramatic backdrop for the dusting of rose petals and flickering silver candles. This was the culmination of Chase's and his mother's efforts, along with those of an amazing team of volunteers.

Chase escorted Kay into the room, and she took in what the town had accomplished. "This place will help so many."

"I only wish Daddy was here to see it," Chase added. "He would have loved to be a part of this."

"I know he would have." Kay rested her head against her son's shoulder. "And I hope one day we can clear your father's name, removing any doubt. I haven't told any of you this, but I remember the day your father finally acquired those mineral rights. After all that time Joe finally had a piece of Scott David, and I wondered how he'd done it. I even asked him if it was on the level, and he swore to me that it was. Now I have two choices. Either continue to believe my husband, who's no longer here to defend himself, or accept that he deceived an elderly man. Either way, love and understanding come into play."

Across the room Chase spotted Nola standing with her family. She was wearing a black sleeveless dress and her hair was gracefully swept up, exposing her delicate neck. She'd never looked more beautiful. He wanted to take her in his arms and tell her how he felt about her. But now wasn't the time. They'd have their moment later tonight. He'd make certain of it.

WHEN EVERYONE WAS seated for dinner, Kay stepped onto the makeshift stage at the front of the room. She looked regal as she gazed over the crowd in her breathtaking emerald-green gown.

"Words cannot begin to express the gratitude I feel toward all of you. Your generous support and contributions created this very room. You made this. All of you, together as one. And even when we're long gone, this building will remain as a reminder to always lend a helping hand to your neighbor. Thank you."

Cole escorted his mother back to the table and Chase took the stage. Looking devilishly handsome in his black tuxedo, he cleared his throat and smiled at Kay.

"My mother and father have always been excellent role models for my brothers and me, and even today, my mother is still teaching us life lessons. She said something to me earlier—when you're faced with a choice, love and understanding come into play." Chase's eyes found Nola's. "She's right. It's something we don't see enough of in this world, and if we all took a step back when faced with a difficult decision and applied a little love and understanding, I think we might see things more clearly. Life isn't black-and-white. Everyone has a past, and we all need to work together to build our futures. None of us is perfect—we're perfectly flawed. And once we learn to accept our differences and come together, we can create the most beautiful of families. Thank you for coming together in support of the Ramblewood Food Bank and this great community it serves."

Nola wanted to run to his side and tell him what she'd discovered—to tell him everything was all right. But he disappeared moments after his speech, probably getting things ready for the auction.

Today felt as if it had been an ongoing battle to catch up with Chase and Nola knew of only one way to get his attention this evening. It couldn't fail.

CHASE WAS EXHAUSTED. He wanted nothing more than to call it a day, take Nola by the hand and go someplace private where they could talk. No interruptions. He wanted to tell her how he truly felt. There were only a few hours left until all the day's events were over, and then he'd have his chance. Right now, it was his turn on the auction block.

"Ladies and gentlemen, we have Chase Langtry, owner of the Ride 'em High! Rodeo School, and he's offering one month of personal rodeo training. Bidding begins at one hundred dollars."

"Dad, please. I want to go to the rodeo school," cried a preteen boy who was sitting near Nola.

The father held his finger to his lips, shaking his head. "No, son, we can't afford it."

The auctioneer began. "One hundred dollar bid, now two, now two, will ya gimme two?"

"Five thousand." Nola stood, and a blush crept into her cheeks as the whispers became a dull roar. Taking a few steps forward, she stood next to the father and the preteen. She placed a hand on the boy's shoulders. "For him. The lessons are for him if you'll give me this time—right now—to hear me out.

Chase froze in place on the stage, afraid to move. A KWTT camera crew made their way toward the front of the room, startling Nola at first. Then she laughed.

"That figures. After covering the news for years now I am the news." She cleared her throat. "I've been trying to tell you this all day, Chase, but you've been a hard man to catch up with. I received a phone call today from a woman who visits Nate David on a regular basis. He was a good friend of her father's, and when her father died, she continued to look in on Nate daily. She told me that while Nate had been diagnosed with Alzheimer's seven years ago, he was only in the early stages of the disease back then. Three years later it had progressed to where it began to affect his day-to-day activities and he hired a live-in caregiver. He had been lucid and in control of his faculties up until he went into a nursing home last year. Nate spent many birthdays and holidays with her family and she has home-video footage from those occasions that prove that Nate was of sound mind at the time of the sale. He actually discusses the sale on one of the videos. Joe Langtry is one hundred percent innocent, and this woman will testify to that."

"Oh, my." Kay stood and walked toward Nola. "You've done it. You've cleared my husband's name."

"I had help." Nola bobbed her head. "A whole team of my own, but yes, Joe's name is clear."

The audience she'd forgotten about began to clap as Chase stepped off the stage and made his way toward her.

"Thank you." Chase pulled her into his arms. Lifting her chin, he gently placed a kiss on her lips. "You have no idea what you've done for my family."

Reclaiming her lips once more, Chase crushed Nola to him, wishing the moment would never end.

Chapter Thirteen

"Mom." Cole stood and motioned for everyone to gather around the Langtry living room. "We wanted to do this at the Mistletoe Rodeo, but we know how you get about having attention on you in public, so we decided to wait until it was just us family."

"Grandma." Ever handed Kay a plaque. "This is from all of us. We love you and appreciate you, every day of our lives."

Tears spilled onto Kay's cheeks as she accepted the gift. A red enamel rose adorned the top. It was a replica of the red rose she wore on a pendant around her neck—a gift from Joe on their first wedding anniversary. She wiped her eyes and read the plaque aloud. *"Kay Langtry. We wouldn't be a family without you.* Oh, my word, it has all of your names on it, too. Thank you. Thank you all so much."

Chase couldn't believe Christmas was only a few days away and Nola was standing beside him. After yesterday's Mistletoe Rodeo, Kay had asked her and her family to join them for tonight's dinner. He and Nola still hadn't had the chance to talk privately, but after their very public gestures to one another at the Mistletoe Rodeo, Chase finally felt as if things were falling into place.

Nola wasn't the only visitor they were expecting that evening. And Chase wasn't quite sure how to react considering the man almost cost them—him—everything.

Earlier in the day, Clay Tanner had discovered the geological study Joe had ordered shortly after he had purchased the mineral rights. It matched the one Scott David had commissioned a few months ago. There was nothing under Nate David's fifty thousand acres. It had been a bum investment on Joe's part, one meant to teach Scott David a lesson.

When Jon contacted Scott about the geological study and video proof Nola had uncovered, the man broke down, saying all he had ever wanted was to have his family's land back intact. He admitted to making numerous mistakes when he had first gone into business, including ruthlessly going up against Joe whenever possible. The land had been the David family's original homestead and Scott wanted to retain that legacy for his own children. Shortly before his grandfather had gone into the nursing home, Scott had discovered the mineral rights had been sold to none other than Joe Langtry and it had become personal.

Scott had asked if he could apologize in person, and that was when Kay had asked him to join them for dinner.

He wasn't at all what they had expected when he arrived. The photographs of him online looked cold and even menacing at times, but Scott was an extremely personable and very well-read man. The woman they had called his trophy wife wore the pants in the family. Juanita was as kind as she was beautiful, insisting that she help in the kitchen before, during and after dinner.

Once everyone relaxed, they realized Scott wasn't that different from them.

"I didn't mean to put you through so much hell." Scott sat on the couch next to Kay. "My family is my world. Pop and I had a strained relationship at best. We never saw eye to eye on anything business related. When he went into the nursing home and I found out he'd been diagnosed with Alzheimer's I was livid. Mainly because I hadn't known, but also because I thought my enemy had taken advantage of my father. I never should have handled it the way I did."

Kay held his hand in hers. "We've all made mistakes. My boys and I could have ended this by offering you the mineral rights before this ever escalated. We were just as stubborn as you were. And heaven knows my Joe was no saint. He never should have gone after those mineral rights in the first place. We've decided collectively as a family to sell them to you for one dollar. The way I see it, we're fixing a long-overdue wrong. It's our gift to you in the spirit of Christmas."

Scott's face became flushed. "That's very generous of you, but I'd like to pay you what Joe paid for them. I know they're worth substantially less since the geological survey indicates nothing of value beneath the land. But I insist."

"Scott, just say Merry Christmas," Kay said.

"Merry Christmas."

NOLA FOUND HERSELF on the verge of tears once again. The Langtrys and their Hallmark moments got her every time. Excusing herself to the front porch, Nola sat in one of the antique rockers, looking onto the pecan grove of twinkling lights.

"And finally we're alone." Chase stepped out onto the porch.

Nola pulled her jacket tighter around her without looking up. "I was just thinking that this is where it all began. I think I knew then how much you were about to mean to me. As much as I didn't want to admit it." Chase was close enough for her to touch, and as much as she ached for him, she was equally afraid. "Would you believe I had two job offers today? One from News Channel 16 and KWTT once again offering me the co-anchor position. I lost you because of that job. It's not worth it. I don't want to report the news anymore."

"What do you want?" Chase's voice was barely louder than a whisper.

"I want to go back to school and follow the dream I had when I was a kid—to be a translator. I have no idea where to even begin, but I think now is a really good time to find out. I've always done what I was told to do. It feels good to actually think for myself for a change."

Chase stood in front of her and gently pulled Nola to her feet, the heat of his touch almost causing her to sag against him. "Tell me what else you want."

"I want to live." Nola stroked his cheek with the back of her fingers. "I want to experience life…with you by my side."

"I want the same thing, Nola." Chase brushed a strand of hair from her face. "I know you don't want children and that's been a real battle for me, but I'm not without children. I have my niece, nephews and all my rodeo school kids. Family isn't just about DNA, and I'm sorry I didn't accept that sooner. I tried living without you and I failed miserably. I love you, Nola. I don't want to spend a single day without you. And if that means no kids of our own, I can live with it."

Nola couldn't believe the words coming out of his mouth. Chase was willing to make the ultimate sacrifice…for her. It touched her very soul, and she'd never felt more loved in her entire life.

"What if I said you didn't have to?"

"What are you saying?" Chase searched her face imploringly.

"After spending time around your family, I like the idea of having one of my own, but that's only if you're willing to explore all of our options."

"Yes, Nola, yes."

"I love you, Chase Langtry. Thank you for giving me the gift of family this Christmas."

"I love you, too. Merry Christmas."

* * * * *

A HOME FOR CHRISTMAS

Laura Marie Altom

"Rachel!"

Ignoring Chance Mulgrave, her husband's best friend, Rachel Finch gripped her umbrella handle as if it were the only thing keeping her from throwing herself over the edge of the cliff, at the base of which thundered an angry Pacific. Even for Oregon Coast standards, the day was hellish. Brutal winds, driving cold rain...

The wailing gloom suited her. Only ten minutes earlier, she'd left the small chapel where her presumed dead husband's memorial service had just been held.

"Please, Rachel!" Chance shouted above the storm. Rachel didn't see Chance since her back was to him, but she could feel him thumping toward her on crutches. "Honey..."

He cupped his hand to her shoulder and she flinched, pulling herself free of his hold. "Don't."

"Sure," he said. "Whatever. I just—"

She turned to him, too exhausted to cry. "I'm pregnant."

"What?"

"Wes didn't know. I'd planned on telling him after he'd finished this case."

"God, Rache." Sharing the suffocating space beneath her umbrella, his demeanor softened. "I'm sorry. Or maybe happy. Hell, I'm not sure what to say."

"There's not much anyone can say at this point," she responded. "Wes is gone. I'm having his child… but how can I even think of being a mother when I'm so emotionally…"

"Don't worry about a thing," he said. "No matter what you need, I'm here for you. Wes and I made a pact. Should anything happen to either of us, we'd watch after each other's family."

"But you don't have a family," she pointed out.

"Yet. But it could've just as easily been me whose life we were celebrating here today." He bowed his head. "Seeing you like this…so sad…makes me almost wish it was."

Me, too.

There. Even if Rachel hadn't given voice to her resentment, it was at least out there, for the universe to hear. Ordinarily, Chance and her husband worked together like a well-oiled team, watching each other's backs. But then Chance had had to go and bust his ankle while helping one of their fellow deputy US marshals move into a new apartment.

If Chance had really cared for Wes, he'd have been more careful. He wouldn't have allowed his friend to be murdered at the hands of a madman—a rogue marshal who'd also come uncomfortably close to taking out one of the most key witnesses the Marshal's Service had ever had.

Her handful of girlfriends had tried consoling her, suggesting maybe Wes wasn't really dead…but Rachel knew. There had been an exhaustive six-week search for Wes's body. Combined with that, of the five marshals who'd been on that assignment, only two had come home alive. Another two bodies had been found, both shot. It didn't take rocket science to assume the same had happened to her dear husband.

"Let me take you home," Chance said. Despite his crutches, he tried to angle her away from the thrashing sea and back to the parking lot, to the sweet little chapel where less than a year earlier she and Wes had spoken their wedding vows.

"You're soaked. Being out here in this weather can't be good for you or the baby."

"I'm all right," she said, again wrenching free of his hold. This time, it had been her elbow he'd grasped. She was trying to regain her dignity after having lost it in front of the church filled with Wes's coworkers and friends, and she just wanted to be left alone. "Please…leave. I can handle this on my own."

"Rachel, that's just it," he said, awkwardly chasing after her as she strode down the perilous trail edging the cliff.

His every step tore at her heart. Why was he alive and not her husband? The father of her child. What was she going to do? How was she ever going to cope with raising a baby on her own?

"Honey, you don't have to deal with Wes's passing

on your own. If you'd just open up to me, I'm here for you—for as long as you need."

That was the breaking point. Rachel stopped abruptly. She tossed her umbrella out to sea, tipped her head up to the battering rain and screamed.

Tears returned with a hot, messy vengeance. Only, in the rain it was impossible to tell where tears left off and rain began. Then, suddenly, Chance was there, drawing her against him, into his island of strength and warmth, his crutches braced on either side of her like walls blocking the worst of her pain.

"That's it," he crooned into her ear. "Let it out. I'm here. I'm here."

She did exactly as he urged, but then, because she'd always been an intensely private person and not one prone to histrionics, she stilled. Curiously, the rain and wind also slowed to a gentle patter and hushed din.

"Thank you," she eventually said. "You'll never know how much I appreciate you trying to help, but…"

"I'm not just trying," he said. "If you'd let me in, we can ride this out together. I'm hurting, too."

"I know," she said, looking to where she'd white-knuckle gripped the soaked lapels of his buff-colored trench. "But I—I can't explain. I have to do this on my own. I was alone before meeting Wes, and now I am again."

"But you don't have to be. Haven't you heard a word I've said? I'm here for you."

"No," she said, walking away from him again, this time in the direction of her car.

"Thanks, but definitely, no."

Eighteen months later...

THROUGH THE RAIN-DRIZZLED, holiday-themed windows of bustling Hohlmann's Department Store, Chance caught sight of a woman's long, buttery-blond hair. Heart pounding, his first instinct was to run toward her, seeking an answer to the perpetual question: Was it her? Was it Rachel?

No. It wasn't her. And this time, just as so many others, the disappointment landed like a crushing blow to his chest.

That day at the chapel had been the last time he'd seen her. Despite exhaustive efforts to track her, she'd vanished—destroying him inside and out.

When eventually he'd had to return to work and his so-called normal life, he'd put a private investigator on retainer, telling the man to contact him upon finding the slightest lead.

"You all right?" his little sister, nineteen-year-old Sarah, asked above an obnoxious Muzak rendition of "Jingle Bells." She was clutching the prewrapped perfume box she'd just purchased for their mother. "You look like you've seen a ghost."

"Might as well have," he said, taking the box from her to add to his already bulging bag. "Got everything you need?"

"Sure," she said, giving him the *Look*. The one

that said she knew he was thinking about Rachel again, and that her wish for Christmas was that her usually wise big brother would once and for all put the woman—his dead best friend's wife—out of his heart and head.

Two hours later, Chance stuck his key in the lock of the Victorian relic his maternal grandmother had left him, shutting out hectic holiday traffic and torrential rain. Portland had been swamped under six inches in the past twenty-four hours. The last time they'd had such a deluge had been the last time he'd seen Rachel.

"Where are you?" he asked softly as the wind bent gnarled branches, eerily scratching them against the back porch roof.

Setting his meager selection of family gifts on the wood bench parked alongside the door, he looked away from the gray afternoon and to the blinking light on his answering machine. Expecting the message to be from Sarah, telling him she'd left a gift or glove in his Jeep, he pressed Play.

"Chance," his PI said, voice like gravel from too many cigarettes and not enough broccoli. "I've got a lead for you on that missing Finch girl. It's a long shot, but you said you wanted everything, no matter how unlikely…"

Despite the fact that Rachel had run off without the decency of a proper—or even improper—goodbye, her tears still haunted him when he closed his eyes.

Chance listened to the message three times before

committing the information to memory, then headed to his computer to book a flight to Denver.

"WESLEY, SWEETIE, PLEASE stop crying," Rachel crooned to her ten-month-old baby boy, the only bright spot in what was becoming an increasingly frightening life. Having grown up in an orphanage, Rachel was no stranger to feeling alone in a crowd, or having to make it on her own. So why, after six months, was this still so hard?

Despite her hugging and cooing, the boy only wailed more.

"Want me to take him?"

She looked up to see one of Baker Street Homeless Shelter's newest residents wave grungy hands toward her child. She hadn't looked much better when she'd first arrived, and Rachel still couldn't get past the shock that she and her baby were now what most people would call *bums*.

After reverting back to the name she'd gone by at the orphanage, Rachel Parkson, she'd traveled to Denver to room with her friend Jenny. But while Jenny had gotten lucky, landing a great job transfer to Des Moines, Rachel had descended into an abyss of bad luck.

A tough pregnancy had landed her in hospital. While she'd been blessed with a beautiful, healthy baby, at the rate she was going, the hefty medical bill wouldn't be gone till he was out of high school. Wes's life insurance company had repeatedly denied her claim, stating that without a body it wouldn't pay.

Making a long, sad story short, she'd lost everything, and here she was, now earning less than minimum wage doing bookkeeping for the shelter while trying to finish her business degree one night course at a time through a downtown Denver community college.

She was raising her precious son in a shelter with barely enough money for diapers, let alone food and a place of their own. She used to cry herself to sleep every night, but now, she was just too exhausted. She used to pray, as well, but it seemed God, just like her husband, had deserted her.

Baby Wesley continued to wail.

"Sorry for all the noise," she said to the poor soul beside her, holding her son close as she wearily pushed to her feet with her free hand. She had to get out of here, but how? How could she ever escape this downward financial spiral?

"Rachel?"

That voice…

She paused before looking up. But when she did, tingles climbed her spine.

"Chance?"

AFTER ALL THIS TIME, was it really Rachel? Raising Wes's child in a homeless shelter? Why, why hadn't she just asked for help?

Chance pressed the heel of his hand to stinging eyes.

"Y-you look good," he said, lying through his teeth at the waiflike ghost of the woman he used to know.

Dark shadows hollowed pale blue eyes. Wes used to brag about the silky feel of Rachel's long hair cascading against his chest when they'd made love—but it was now shorn into a short cap. "And the baby. He's wonderful, Rachel. You did good."

"Thanks," she said above her son's pitiful cry. "We're okay." She paused. "What are you doing here?"

"I'm here to see you… To help you…"

"I don't need help."

"Bull," he said, taking the now screaming baby from her, cradling him against his chest, nuzzling the infant's downy hair beneath his chin. "What's his name?"

"Wesley," she said, refusing to meet his gaze.

He nodded, fighting a sudden knot at the back of his throat. Such a beautiful child, growing up in such cruel surroundings. And why? All because of Rachel's foolish pride.

"Get your things," he growled between clenched teeth, edging her away from a rag-clothed derelict reeking of booze.

"W-what?"

"You heard me. You tried things your way, honey, and apparently it didn't work out. Now we're doing it *my* way. Your husband's way."

"I— I'm fine," she said, raising her chin, a partial spark back in her stunning eyes. "Just a little down on my luck. But things will change. They'll get better."

"Damn straight they will." Clutching the infant with one arm, he dragged her toward the shelter's door with the other. "You don't want charity from me, fine. But is this really what you want for your son? Wes's son?"

While Chance regretted the harshness of his words, he'd never retract them. Years ago he'd made a promise to her husband, and he sure as hell wasn't about to back out on it now.

He glanced away from Rachel to take in a nearly bald, fake Christmas tree that'd been decorated with homemade ornaments. Pipe cleaner reindeer and paper angels colored with crayons. Though the tree's intent was kind, he knew Rachel deserved better.

While killing time on endless stakeouts, Wes would ramble for hours about his perfect wife. About how much he loved her, how she was a great cook, how she always managed to perfectly balance the checkbook. Wes went so far as to offer private morsels he should've kept to himself—locker room details that should've been holy between a man and his wife. But because of Wes's ever-flapping mouth, whether he'd wanted to or not, Chance knew everything about Rachel from her favorite songs to what turned her on.

Another thing he knew were Wes's dreams for her. How because she'd grown up in an orphanage, he'd always wanted to have a half-dozen chubby babies with her and buy her a great house and put good, reliable tires on her crappy car.

Chance had made a promise to his best friend; one that put him in charge of picking up where Wes left off. It was a given he'd steer clear of the husband-wife physical intimacies—she was off-limits. Totally. But when it came to making her comfortable, happy…by God, if it took every day for the rest of his life, that's what Chance had come to Denver prepared—and okay, he'd admit it, secretly hoping—to do.

Looking back to Rachel, he found her eyes pooled. Lips trembling, she met his stare.

"Come on," he said. "It's time to go home."

Baby Wesley had fallen asleep in Chance's arms. His cheeks were flushed, and he sucked pitifully at his thumb.

"I—I tried breastfeeding him," she said. "But my milk dried up."

"That happens," he said, not knowing if it did or didn't or why she'd even brought it up…just willing to say anything to get her to go with him.

Shaking her head, looking away to brush tears, she said, "Wait here. I'll get our things."

FOR RACHEL, BEING at the airport and boarding the plane was surreal. As was driving through a fog-shrouded Portland in Chance's Jeep, stopping off at an all-night Walmart for a car seat and over five hundred dollars' worth of clothes, diapers, formula and other baby supplies. The Christmas decorations, hundreds and thousands of colorful lights lining each new street they traveled, struck her as foreign. As if from a world where she was no longer welcome.

"I'll repay you," she said from the passenger seat, swirling a pattern in the fogged window. Presumably, he was heading toward his lovely hilltop home she'd always secretly called the real estate version of a wedding cake. "For everything. The clothes. Plane ticket. I'll pay it all back. I—I just need a breather to get back on my feet."

"Sure," he said. Was it her imagination, or had he tightened his grip on the wheel?

"Really," she said, rambling on about how Wes's life insurance company refused to pay. "Just as soon as I get the check, I'll reimburse you."

"Know how you can pay me?" he asked, pressing the garage door remote on the underbelly of his sun visor.

She shook her head.

He pulled the Jeep into the single-stall detached garage she'd helped Wes and him build, that same enchanted summer she and her future husband had become lovers.

It is said a woman's heart is a deep well of secrets and Rachel knew hers was no different. Squeezing her eyes shut, she saw Chance as she had that first night they'd met at Ziggy's Sports Bar—before she'd even met Wes. Despite his physical appearance— six-three, with wide, muscular shoulders and a chest as broad and strong as an oak's trunk—Chance's shy, kind spirit made him a gentle giant to whom she'd instinctively gravitated.

Never the brazen type, Rachel had subtly asked mutual friends about him, and every so often, when their eyes met from opposite ends of the bar during the commercial breaks of *Monday Night Football*, she'd thought she'd caught a glimmer of interest. And if only for an instant, hope that he might find her as attractive as she found him would soar. But then he'd look away and the moment would be gone.

Then she'd met Wes—who'd made it known in about ten exhilaratingly sexy seconds that he didn't just want to be her *friend*. Handsome, five-eleven with a lean build and quick smile, Wes hadn't had to work too hard to make her fall for him—or to make any and all occasions magic.

Chance turned off the engine and sighed. The only light was that which spilled from the weak bulb attached to the automatic opener, the only sounds those of rain pattering the roof and the baby's sleepy gurgle… Angling on his seat, Chance reached out to Rachel, whispering the tip of his index finger so softly around her lips…she might've imagined his being there at all.

"Know how you can repay me?" he repeated.

Heartbeat a sudden storm, she swallowed hard.

"By bringing back your smile."

RACHEL AWOKE THE next morning to unfamiliar softness, and the breezy scent of freshly laundered sheets. Sunshine streamed through tall paned windows. After a moment of initial panic, fearing she may have died and moved on to heaven, she remembered herself not on some random cloud, but safely tucked in Chance's guest bed in the turret-shaped room she'd urged him to paint an ethereal sky blue.

The room was the highest point in his home, reached by winding stairs, and its view never failed to stir her. Mt. Hood was to the west, while to the east—

long ago, while standing on a ladder, paint brush in hand, nose and cheeks smudged blue—she'd sworn she could see all the way to the shimmering Pacific. Wesley and Chance had laughed at her, but she'd ignored them.

To Rachel, the room represented freedom from all that had bound her in her early, depressing, pre-Wes life. The panoramic views, just as her marriage, made her feel as if her soul was flying.

As she inched up in the sumptuous feather bed to greet a day as chilly as it was clear, the room still wielded its calming effect. She'd awakened enough to realize how late it must be…and yet Wesley hadn't stirred.

Tossing back covers, she winced at the wood floor's chilly bite against her bare feet. With one look at the portable crib that had been among their purchases the previous night, Rachel realized that Wesley's cries hadn't woken her because he wasn't there.

Bounding to the kitchen, she found her son sitting proud in his new high chair, beaming, covered ear to ear in peachy-smelling orange goo.

"Morning, sleepyhead." Baby spoon to Wesley's cooing lips, Chance caught her off guard with the size of his smile.

"You should've woken me," she said, hustling to where the two guys sat at a round oak table in a sunny patch of the country kitchen. "I'm sure you have better things to do."

"Nope," he said. "I took the day off."

"I'll pay you for your time."

He'd allowed her to take the spoon as she'd pulled out a chair and sat beside him, but now, his strong fingers clamped her wrist. "Stop."

"What?"

"The whole defensive routine. It doesn't become you."

"S-sorry. That's who I am."

"Bull."

"E-excuse me?" He released her, and the spoon now trembled in her still tingling wrist.

"I knew you as playful. Fun. Now, you seem like you're in attack mode."

"And why shouldn't I be?" she asked. "Aside from Wesley, name one thing that's gone right for me in the past year?"

"That's easy," he said, cracking a slow and easy grin that, Lord help her, had Rachel's pulse racing yet again. Had the man always been this attractive?

Judging by the massive crush she'd had on him all those years ago…yes.

Making things worse—or better, depending how you looked at it—he winked. "One thing that's gone very right is how you're finally back with me."

SENSING RACHEL NEEDED two gifts above all else that Christmas season—time and space—Chance returned to work Tuesday, and every day for the rest of the week. Come Saturday, though, despite her protests that they should stay at the house, he bustled her and the baby into his Jeep and started off for the traditional holiday ride he'd loved as a kid, but had given up as an adult.

"Well?" he asked a silent Rachel an hour later, pulling into a snow-covered winter wonderland. "See anything that'd fit in the living room bay window?"

She glanced at him, then at the sprawling Christmas tree farm that might as well have been Santa's North Pole as everywhere you looked, Christmas was in full swing. Kids laughing and sledding and playing tag while darting in and out amongst fragrant trees. Families hugging the fires built in river rock pits, sipping steaming mugs of cocoa. Upbeat carols played from a tiny speaker.

"It's—" she cautiously glanced at the idyllic scene before them, as if they didn't belong, then back to him "—amazing. But if you want a tree, wouldn't it be cheaper to—"

"Look—" he sighed "—I wasn't going to bring this up until it's a done deal, but I told my boss about your situation—with Wes's flaky life insurance—and fury didn't begin to describe his reaction. Wheels are turning, and I'd say you'll have a check by the end of next week."

"Really?"

Just then, she was seriously gorgeous, eyes brimming with hope and a shimmering lake of tears. "Yeah," Chance said. "I'm serious. So what's with the waterworks? I thought you'd be thrilled to be rich?"

"I would be—I mean, I am. It's just that after all these months of barely scraping by, not sleeping because I've literally been afraid to close my eyes, it seems a bit surreal to have such a happy ending at all, let alone in such a happy place."

He laughed, unfastening his seat belt to grab the baby from his seat. "Don't you think after what you've been through you two deserve a little happiness?"

She turned away from him while she sniffled and dried her cheeks, and he couldn't tell if she was nodding or shaking her head. "Well?" he asked. "Was that a yes or no?"

"I don't know," she said with a laugh. "Maybe both. I'm just so confused. And grateful. Very, *very* grateful."

"Yeah, well, what you need to be," he said, Wesley snug in his arms, "is energized."

"Oh, yeah?" she asked, again blasting him with a tremulous smile. "How come?"

"Because me and this kid of yours are about to *whomp* you in a snowball fight."

"IT'S BEAUTIFUL," RACHEL SAID, stepping back to admire the nine-foot fir they'd finished decorating. Heirloom glass ornaments and twinkling white lights hung from each branch. "Perfect."

With Chance beside her, carols softly playing and a fire crackling in the hearth, Rachel couldn't have ordered a more enchanting holiday scene.

"I don't know," Chance said, finger to his lips as he stood beside her, surveying their afternoon's work. "Something's missing."

"You're right," Rachel said. "We forgot the angel."

"I didn't see it, did you?"

"Not in the boxes we've been through. Maybe—"
She looked down to see Wesley sucking the top corner of the angel's box. "Aha! Found it."

"Thanks, bud." Chance took the box from the baby, replacing it with the teething ring he had been contentedly gumming. "How about you do the honors?" he suggested, handing the golden angel to her.

"I'd like that," Rachel said, embarrassed to admit just how much the small gesture meant.

At the orphanage, placing the angel on top of the tree was generally a task reserved for the child who was newest to the home. Since Rachel had gone to live there the summer just before her fourth birthday when her parents had been killed in a car accident, she'd never had the chance. By the time Christmas rolled around, she had only been the third-newest kid.

Knowing this, Wes had made their first Christmas together as a married couple extra special by taking her to pick out an especially extravagant angel that they really couldn't afford. In Denver, at a desperation yard sale she'd held in a futile attempt to stay financially afloat, it had devastated her to have to sell that precious angel to a cranky old guy for the princely sum of three dollars.

Rachel swallowed hard at the bittersweet memory of how dearly she'd loved sharing Christmas with Wes. There was a part of her struggling with the guilt that she was once again immersed in holiday cheer… but Wes was gone. It somehow felt disloyal for her to be so happy.

Trying to focus on the task at hand, Rachel climbed

onto the small stepladder she'd used to hang the ornaments from the highest branches, but she still wasn't
tall enough to reach the tree's top.

"Let me help," Chance said, inching up behind her,
settling his hands around her waist, then lifting her
the extra inches needed to get the job done.

His nearness was overwhelming, flooding her
senses to the point she nearly failed her mission. Had
his hands lingered on her waist longer than necessary
after he'd set her back to her feet? Was that the reason for her erratically beating heart? What kind of
woman was she to one minute reminisce about her
deceased husband, and the next wonder at the feel of
another man's strong hands?

"Thank you," she said, licking her lips, going by
habit to push back her long hair that was no longer
there.

"You're welcome." As if he'd sensed the awareness between them, too, they both fell into awkward
step, bustling to clean the wreckage of tissue paper
and boxes.

Once they'd finished hauling the mess to a spare
bedroom Chance used for storage, they were in the
dark upstairs hall when Chance asked, "Why'd you
cut your hair?"

The question caught her off guard, made her feel
even more uncomfortable than she already did. "It
was too much trouble," she said.

"It was beautiful. Not that it's any of my business,
but you should grow it back."

She looked down to hands she'd clenched at her waist.

"Not that you aren't still attractive," he said. "It's just that Wes always had a thing for your hair. I think he'd be sad to see it gone."

What about you, Chance? Did you like my hair?

Rachel was thankful for the hall's lack of light— the question, even if asked only in her head, made her uncomfortable. Why would she even care what Chance thought of the way she used to style her hair? Worse yet, why did his question leave her feeling lacking?

Suddenly, she was wishing she at least had a little more length to work into an attractive style instead of the boyish cut that'd been easy to keep clean and neat at the homeless shelter. This cut hardly made her feel feminine or desirable. But then until her reunion with Chance, she'd had no use for vanity.

"Chance?" she asked, her voice a croaked whisper.

"Yes?"

"When we first met, you know, back when you, me and Wes used to just be friends, hanging out at Ziggy's, did you find me pretty?"

He cleared his throat. "What kind of question is that?"

"I don't know." She shook her head. "Sorry I asked."

Because she truly didn't know, Rachel returned to the living room, where holiday cheer and the sight of her contented child banished doubts and fears. The question had been silly. As was her growing aware- ness of her late husband's best friend. For a moment she felt better, but then Chance returned, his essence filling the room.

"For the record," he said, perching alongside her on the toasty fireplace hearth, "yes. I thought you were pretty back then, but you're even prettier now."

CHANCE HAD A tough time finding sleep. Why had Rachel asked him such a loaded question? Why did he feel his final, almost flirty answer had been a betrayal of his friend's trust? Yeah, Chance thought she was pretty—gorgeous, in fact. But for Wes's sake, couldn't he have just skirted the issue?

Sunday morning, he woke to a breakfast spread fit for a five-star hotel. "Wow," he said. "What's all this for?"

Looking more gorgeous than any woman had a right to first thing in the morning, she shrugged. "Guess I just wanted to say thanks for the great day we had yesterday. Never having had a family growing up, I always wished for that kind of traditional family fun."

"Is that what we are?" he asked, forking a bite of pancake. "A family?"

"You know what I mean," she said, avoiding his glance by drinking orange juice.

He broke off a piece of bacon and handed it to Wesley.

"Yeah," he said. "I know what you mean. But *is* that what we are, Rache?"

Sitting with her and Wesley, from out of nowhere Chance was struck with the realization that no matter how she answered his question, he very much *wanted* them to be a family. They'd already fallen into husband and wife roles. The only things missing were emotional and physical closeness.

And as reluctant as he was to admit it, from the day he'd set eyes on her all those years ago, kissing Rachel was something he'd always longed to do. And therein lay the rub. Somehow, he had to find it within himself to squelch that want.

"We're sort of a family," she said. "But I suppose, once I get Wes's life insurance you'll probably be glad to get the house back to yourself."

Boldly reaching across the table for her hand, stroking her palm, lying to himself by labeling it a casual, friendly touch, he said, "Actually, it's nice having you two here. Waking up to you in the morning, coming home to you at night."

She laughed off his admission. "You're just being polite. No bachelor actually enjoys being strapped with another man's wife and child."

"That's just it," he said. "Crazy as it may seem, I like you being here—a lot."

ANOTHER WEEK PASSED, during which Rachel had too much time to ponder Chance's curious statement. He liked having her and Wesley sharing his house? If only he truly felt that way because, truth be told, she liked being there, and judging by Wesley's easy grins, he did, too.

Being with Chance made her feel safe—an emotion that'd been sorely lacking from the past eighteen months of her life. Being with him now told her what a fool she'd been for ever denying his offer of help and companionship. He was a wonderful man.

The only reason she was now standing at the front window on a sunny Friday afternoon, watching for his Jeep to head up the winding lane leading to his home was because she was thankful to him…right? No way could it be something more.

Trouble was, try as she might to pass off the growing feelings she had for him as simply affection between friends, she *did* feel something more. Twinges of attraction. Flickering flames.

Whatever the label, it had wrongfully been there Sunday morning when he'd held her hand across the breakfast table. And Monday night when their hands brushed while Chance helped with Wesley's bath. Again still Tuesday and Wednesday when they'd shared the usually dull duty of cleaning up after dinner.

Instead of being ho-hum, washing dishes with Chance towering beside her, making her feel small and cherished and protected, had been—in a word— *intoxicating*.

But why? Why couldn't she keep at the forefront of her mind the fact that Chance had been Wes's best friend? To follow through on any attraction for him would be wrong.

Finally, she saw him pulling into the drive. Though she wanted to run to the back door to greet him like a giddy school girl, she somehow managed to rein in her emotions. Instead, with Wesley in her arms, she checked on the latest fragrant batch of sugar cookies still in the oven.

"Smells wonderful in here," Chance said with a gorgeous grin on his way through the back door. "You must be psychic."

"Why's that?" she asked, telling herself the heat from the oven had her cheeks flushed—not the pleasure of being the recipient of his smile.

"My parents invited us for dinner. Sugar cookies are Dad's favorite—not that he'll need a reason to fall for you or my buddy Wesley." After slipping off his coat, then setting his keys and wallet on the blue tile counter, he took the baby from her, swooping him high into the air, then snug against his chest for a cuddle and kiss. "Mmm... I missed you," he said, nuzzling the infant's head.

Rachel fought irrational jealousy strumming through her as she realized she wanted Chance to have missed her, too. Almost as much as she wanted a welcome home kiss...

RELAXING OVER ALMOND Bundt cake and coffee with Chance's mother, Helen, while the men washed up after dinner, Rachel would've had a hard time remembering a time she'd ever felt more content.

Helen had decorated her home from top to bottom in holiday decor ranging from elegant to goofy fun. The crackling fire and Elvis CD of holiday love songs playing softly in the background only made the night that much more special.

"Please don't think me forward for bringing this

up," Helen said after they'd had a few moments to finish their cake, "but my son's a different person around you and Wesley. Better, in every conceivable way."

Rachel was so caught off guard by the woman's random statement that she darned near choked on her last bite of dessert. "Oh?"

"He loves you, you know. Has loved you ever since you first met all those years ago. Bless his heart…" She paused for a sip of coffee. "He was always the strong, silent type. His father and I urged him to tell you how he felt before you and Wes grew close, but he missed his window of opportunity and seeing how he and Wes were always such good friends, he did the gentlemanly thing and bowed out."

Not knowing what to say, her head and heart reeling, Rachel was hard-pressed to say much else but another "Oh."

"He'd kill me if he knew I was telling you all of this, it's just that—" she peeked over her shoulder to make sure they were alone "—I'm not getting any younger and the thought of having an instant grandson, as well as a daughter-in-law whose company I'm very much enjoying, fills me with indescribable joy."

CHANCE LOVES ME.

Lying in bed that night, listening to Wesley softly snore from the beautiful crib Chance had bought for him on a wondrously hectic shopping trip Tuesday afternoon, Rachel wasn't sure what to do with this knowledge.

Part of her wished Chance's mother had kept her

nose out of her son's affairs. Another part, the part of Rachel increasingly craving Chance's touch, was secretly thrilled. But if she was falling for Chance, what did that say about her love for her poor husband? What kind of wife was she to so soon be falling head over heels for Wes's best friend?

Finding sleep impossible, she tossed back the covers and padded barefoot downstairs. Cookies and milk. That's all she needed to get this ridiculous notion from her head.

She *wasn't* falling for Chance. He was like her brother.

She was grateful to him.

"Hey, gorgeous," he said from in front of the open fridge, the dim light washing over the muscles of his bare chest. "Fancy meeting you here." He winked.

Her mouth went dry. That gratitude she was supposedly feeling for him? One sight of his rock-hard pecs and abs and there was no denying it. She wanted the guy—bad. Not in a friendly way, but in a way she had no business even thinking about, let alone aching to act upon.

"Um, hi," she mumbled, biting her lower lip.

"Want milk?" he asked, wagging the gallon jug.

"Yes, please."

While he poured, she grabbed the foil-wrapped plate of cookies from the kitchen's center island.

They reunited at the kitchen table.

"Why can't you sleep?" he asked.

For a long time, she stayed silent, toying with her cookie. "Truth? You."

Gracing her with a slow, sexy grin that turned her resolve to think of him as a brother to mush, he said, "I'm flattered. At least, I hope I have reason to be."

Swallowing hard, she nodded. Everything about him was good. So why, then, did the realization that she was falling for him hurt so bad?

"Rachel?" Setting his milk glass on the table, he asked, "You okay?"

In a last ditch effort to prove to herself—to both of them—that the two of them as a couple would never work, she blurted, "Kiss me."

Per Rachel's request, Chance did kiss her. At first, softly, reverently. But then, the closer she melded to him, the more he increased his pressure, dizzying her with fervent strokes of his tongue.

And then, just as abruptly as their kiss had begun, it ended with Chance pulling away.

Fingers sliding into the hair at his temples, breathing ragged, he said, "Sorry."

"For what?" she asked, eyes welling with emotion. "That was beautiful. It's been so long since I've felt anything but pain. Your kiss…it was as if somewhere deep inside me, the wall of grief I've been hiding behind has been shattered."

"That's all well and good," he said with a sharp laugh. "But what about Wes? Don't you feel guilty? As if our being attracted to each other is a betrayal of his trust?"

Eyes closed, she took a deep breath. "Honestly," she said, eyes open, facing Chance straight on, "I know how awful it must sound, but from the moment your lips touched mine, all I could think about was you."

TWO DAYS LATER, with Wes's life insurance check safely in the bank and her bills paid, Rachel should've been on top of the world. But as she finished wrapping the last of the presents she'd purchased for Chance and his family, all she really felt was sad. He'd invited her to stay with him through New Year's—longer if she liked—but after their kiss, she was more convinced than ever that maybe what would be best for them both was for her and Wesley to move on.

She'd already caused Chance so much trouble. Why stick around if their attraction would only bring him—not to mention, her—pain?

"You look pretty," he said from the living room door, hands behind his back.

"When's the last time you had your eyes checked? I'm a mess." From the oriental rug where she'd parked herself in front of the fire with a mess of bows, boxes and ribbons, she grinned up at him. Dressed in comfy, but hardly flattering sweats, her short hair sticking out at crazy angles and no makeup, she was sure she'd never looked worse.

"My eyes are fine," he said, wading his way through the mess. "Seeing you like this, so at ease in my home…it's my heart I'm worried about."

"Have you always been such a charmer?" she asked, batting her eyelashes exaggeratedly.

"I don't know, you tell me..." From behind his back, he withdrew a perfect cluster of mistletoe.

With him kneeling beside her, holding the sprig over her head, it would've been rude not to follow through with tradition. Seeing how she'd long since put Wesley to bed, Rachel had no qualms about reaching Chance halfway for a mesmerizing kiss.

"You know," Chance said the next afternoon, Wesley gurgling high on his shoulders as they crunched their way through freshly fallen snow in the neighborhood's park, "at work this afternoon, I had some downtime while the jury was deliberating. I did some thinking."

"'Bout time," Rachel quipped.

Her sassy comment earned her a snowball fight. And like the day at the tree farm, the guys once again got the better of her. Laughing so hard her lungs burned from the cold, she cried, "Stop! I give up!"

"Oh, no," Chance said, setting a bundled Wesley beside him so he could tackle her with both hands. "You don't get to surrender until you apologize."

"Sorry, sorry," she laughingly cried, her foggy breath mingling with his.

He kissed her, and despite the fact they were lying in the snow, she felt warmed inside. Which was wrong. She shouldn't be on fire for this man who was her husband's best friend.

"You're forgiven," he said a few minutes later, when her every defense had been shattered. "Now, back to what I was saying before you so rudely interrupted… I've been thinking about how you said you felt like you should find a place of your own. And then I got to thinking how much I enjoy having you both here. And how big this rambling old house of mine is for just me. And how Wes made me promise to look after you if anything should ever happen to him…"

Heart galloping like a herd of runaway reindeer, Rachel alternately dreaded, yet prayed for what she knew Chance would say next.

"And so, anyway, what would you think of the two of us getting hitched? You could still keep your own room, if that's what you wanted, but at least then it'd be official. Me watching out for you and Wesley, I mean."

Tears of joy and sadness stung her eyes.

"Well?" he asked while she blinked.

"Oh, Chance…" Holding her fingers to her mouth, she tugged off her fuzzy mittens with her teeth, then cupped her hand to his cold, whiskered cheek. "I would love nothing more than to marry you. If only there wasn't so much history between us…"

"Say no more," he said, pushing himself off her. "I understand." Snatching up Wesley, he trudged toward the house, telling her without a single word that he didn't truly understand—at all.

AFTER TURNING DOWN Chance's proposal, to say there was tension between them would've been a major understatement—which was why Rachel sat alone in the kitchen that quiet Christmas Eve morning, scanning apartment ads while Chance had gone off to work.

Sipping cocoa while Wesley crumbled a cookie in his high chair, she was startled when the doorbell rang.

"Chance?" she said, running for the front door, hoping now that he'd had time to think about it, he was okay with her suggestion that they remain just friends.

"Sorry," a well-dressed older man said, clearing his throat. "Are you Rachel Finch?"

"Y-yes." She fingered the pearls Helen had given her at her throat.

After introducing himself as Wes's old boss, he said, "Forgive me for dropping by, especially today of all days, but…there's no easy way to say this… we've, well…your husband's body has been identified. I thought you'd like to have his few personal effects."

WITHIN FIFTEEN MINUTES of Rachel's call, Chance roared his Jeep up his normally quiet street. Yes, he'd been deeply wounded by her turning down his proposal, but that didn't mean he was now going to let her down.

He heard the news through the office grapevine— and he also found out Franks had dropped by to pass the news along to Rachel. Chance fully planned to be by her side as she dealt with it all.

"You okay?" he asked, finding her alone at the kitchen table. She had opened the watertight pouch

Wes had been using as a wallet the day he'd been shot. His gold watch, wedding band and the navy wallet all lay in front of her.

Wes had been the consummate Boy Scout, and he'd also hated boats. Back when they were kids, Chance kept a rowboat on his paternal grandparents' farm pond. One sunny afternoon when they'd been about ten, he and Wes had been out rowing when the boat capsized.

Wes didn't get upset often, but when his prized baseball cards fell in the water, he'd freaked—kind of like when he'd learned he was the only guy from the Portland marshal's office assigned to that unconventional-as-hell mission, trying to protect a witness who'd refused to leave his private island.

Had Wes known there was a chance he wouldn't be coming home?

"Rachel?" She still hadn't answered his question.

Looking shell-shocked, she nodded. "Yeah. I'm all right."

"Where's Wesley?"

"Down for his nap."

Pulling out the chair beside her, he asked, "You sure you don't want to be alone for this?"

She shook her head, and off they went on a journey down memory lane. Wes's driver's license and credit cards, photos and fast-food coupons—all of it was in pristine condition.

In the last pocket was a folded slip of yellow legal paper.

Hands trembling, Rachel opened it. "Oh, God," she said. "It's a note."

"'If you're reading this,'" she read aloud, "'then I'm so sorry, sweetie, but…'" She broke down. "I c-can't do this," she said. "Please, Chance. You read it."

He cleared his throat, continuing where she'd left off.

"'…but I've apparently croaked. I know, I know, right about now you're probably wanting to smack me for trying to find humor in this, but I suppose everybody's gotta go eventually, and unfortunately, it seems my time's up.

That said, you're not allowed to be sad— well, maybe you could mope a little for the first week, or two, but after that, I want to be staring down from Heaven at your beautiful smile. I want you having babies and good times and toasting me whenever the top's popped on a beer.'"

"You do this next part," Chance said, closing stinging eyes. "It's too personal."

She took the letter and read on.

"'By now, Chance has no doubt told you about the promise he made me to always watch over you. But what he probably didn't tell you is how he's always had a secret thing for you. Back when we first started dating, he was too much of a gentleman and friend to stand in the way of me marrying you. If I have died, Rachel, he'd be a good man for you. The best—second only to me. Wink, wink. Be sure and give him a shot at…'"

She paused to catch her breath. "'…winning your heart.'"

Sobbing, Rachel clung to Chance, drinking in his goodness and kindness and strength.

"Shh…" Chance crooned, stroking her short hair.

"Even in death, he put my needs before his own," she said softly, gently setting the letter on the table. "And the timing…of all times for me to have finally gotten his letter, on Christmas Eve. What a gift. Makes you wonder if he's up there, watching over us."

"You doubted it?" Chance teased, sliding Rachel off her chair and onto his lap.

"After the rocky months I've had, I doubted not only Wes, but God."

"Gotta admit," he said, thumb brushing her lower lip. "Having you disappear on me like that—I've had my doubts, too."

"Yet look at us now," she said, resting her head on his shoulder. "Maybe Wes knew that without time and space between us, we'd have both been too loyal to his memory to give each other a try?"

"Whatever the reason," Chance said, "we don't have to feel guilty or pained anymore." He smiled at her, gently. "Now, with Wes's blessing, will you marry me, so that you, me and Wesley can start a family all our own?"

"What do you mean, *start*? I thought we already were a family?"

"Right," he said before a spellbinding kiss. "How could I forget?"

CHRISTMAS MORNING, WESLEY snug between them on the living room sofa, a fire crackling in the hearth and the scent of fresh-baked cinnamon rolls flavoring the air, Rachel opened gift after gift that Chance had secretly stashed in nooks and crannies all over the house.

Later, they'd go to his parents' for Christmas dinner with his sisters and extended family, but for now, it was just the three of them, opening sweaters and perfume and books and china figurines and fishing lures and hats and for Wesley, toys, toys and more toys—most of which Rachel guessed he wouldn't be able to play with until he was three!

Once they'd finished their gift extravaganza and all the wrappings had been cleared, Chance stood beside the Christmas tree and said, "Look, honey, here's another package in this bird's nest, and it's tagged for you."

"Chance," Rachel complained, heading his direction. "You've already given me too much."

"Look here, the label says it's from Santa," he said, holding out a tiny, robin's-egg blue box that screamed Tiffany.

Heart racing, hands trembling, Rachel lifted the lid

to peek inside. "Chance…" Tearing at the sight of the glowing, pear-shaped diamond solitaire, she crushed him in a hug. "It's gorgeous. Yes, I'll marry you!"

"Whoa," he said with a sexy grin, pushing her back and shaking his head. "I don't recall asking anything. This was all Santa's doing."

"Well, then, *Santa*," she said, tilting her head back to talk to the high ceiling, "I accept your proposal."

"Now, wait a minute…" Chance pulled her back into his arms. "Not so fast. I thought the two of us had reached an understanding. Those kisses you gave me last night implied a certain level of intimacy and trust. You can't just make out with me, then leave me for a big jolly guy in a red suit."

"Then what do you suggest?" she asked, standing on her tiptoes to press a kiss to his delicious, cinnamon-flavored lips.

"Just to be safe, you'd better marry me right away."

"Yeah, but do I get to keep the ring?"

He winked. "Why not? With any luck, Mr. Ho Ho Ho will go back to his wife…leaving me plenty of time under the mistletoe with mine."

* * * * *

"You remember when you were home on leave two months ago?"

Hard to forget that weekend in Fort Worth. For two people who'd never been in love and likely never would be, they sure had amazing chemistry.

Oblivious to how much he wanted to hold her lithe, warm body in his arms and make sweet love to her all over again, Poppy persisted on her verbal trip down memory lane. "When we went to the Stork Agency and met Anne Marie?"

"Sure, I remember," Trace said, pausing to take in the sexy fall of Poppy's thick, silky mahogany hair. "Anne Marie was a nice kid." And at seventeen years old, Trace recollected, way too young to be pregnant. That was why she was giving up her children for adoption.

"Well, she's picked us to raise her twins!" Poppy exclaimed.

"Seriously?"

"Yes! Can you believe it?" She paused to catch her breath. "There's only one itty-bitty problem…"

Trace saw the hesitation in Poppy's dark brown eyes. Waited for her to continue.

She inhaled sharply. "She wants us to be married."

Whoa now. That had never been on the table.

Trace swung his feet off the desk and sat forward in his chair. "But she knows we're just friends—" and occasional lovers and constant confidantes, he thought "—who happen to want to be parents together." He thought the two of them had made that abundantly clear.

Poppy folded her arms in front of her, the action plumping up the delectable curve of her breasts beneath her ivory turtleneck. Soberly she nodded, adding, "She still gets that neither of us want to get hitched."

No woman prized her independence more than the outspoken Poppy. For a lot of very different reasons, he felt the same. "But?" he prodded.

"Apparently they didn't expect Anne Marie to choose us…but they wanted to give her a basis for comparison. As it turns out there was another couple that was also in the running, who Anne Marie's mother met and prefers, and they *are* married. But in the end, Anne Marie decided she wants us. On the condition," Poppy reiterated with a beleaguered sigh, "that we get hitched and the kids have the same last name."

Don't miss
LONE STAR TWINS by Cathy Gillen Thacker,
available November 2015 everywhere
Harlequin® American Romance®
books and ebooks are sold.

www.Harlequin.com

HAREXP1015

THE WORLD IS BETTER WITH
Romance

Harlequin has everything from contemporary, passionate and heartwarming to suspenseful and inspirational stories.

Whatever your mood, we have a romance just for you!

Connect with us to find your next great read, special offers and more.

f /HarlequinBooks

🐦 @HarlequinBooks

www.HarlequinBlog.com

www.Harlequin.com/Newsletters

HARLEQUIN®

A *Romance* FOR EVERY MOOD™

www.Harlequin.com